Army of One

Army of One

A. K. Henderson

www.urbanbooks.net

Urban Books, LLC
300 Farmingdale Road, NY-Route 109
Farmingdale, NY 11735

ISBN 13: 978-1-945855-87-0
ISBN 10: 1-945855-87-8

First Mass Market Printing October 2018
First Trade Paperback Printing April 2017
Printed in the United States of America

10 9 8 7 6 5 4 3 2 1

Distributed by Kensington Publishing Corp.
Submit orders to:
Customer Service
400 Hahn Road
Westminster, MD 21157-4627
Phone: 1-800-733-3000
Fax: 1-800-659-243

Prologue

Well, another day in this goofy-ass group home, with these bum-ass niggas and this dumb-ass woman. This is a depressing existence I'm living.

Shamar wrote on his notepad as he sat in his room staring in the mirror on his dresser. He continued writing, hoping to drown out the noise in the background from the other occupants of the house.

Two years in this hell hole has turned me into one desperate nigga. I can't imagine anybody having to live through this. Sometimes I'm actually glad they separated me from the things and people on the west side because I never wanted to have to become the type of dude I'd have to be in order to protect myself from some of the stuff I've seen in the streets. I'd rather be

*locked up in one of them cold cells in Cook
County than to do another year in here.*

Writing was the only thing that could calm
Shamar down when the stress of living in the
group home began to weigh heavily on him. He
was almost out of there and couldn't wait to
go find himself. He figured Mrs. Turner, the
director of the group home, knew how he could
be allowed to leave; but, of course, because he
was only seventeen she wasn't giving up any info.
He knew all he had to do was catch her slippin'.

Shamar was fourteen when an accident killed
his mom and landed his father in prison. The
state got involved because none of the family
would take him in. Mrs. Turner knew Shamar's
father from back in the day, and somehow she
pulled some strings to keep the state from ship-
ping Shamar off to a group home in Indiana. The
only drawback at the time was the fact that he
couldn't contact any other family on his own.

"Man, Joe, I miss the hell out of her," Shamar
said to himself as he examined the bracelet that
once belonged to his mother. It was made of sil-
ver with two charms that draped over the top of
his hand when he wore it. One charm was a small
cross, and the other was a heart. When Shamar
was eight years old, his parents had taken him

to see the place where they had first met. The picture of the two gazing into each other's eyes was ingrained in his mind. His mother, Darlene, wore a small heart on a necklace around her neck. In the same fashion, his father, Shamar Sr., wore a small cross around his neck.

It was midday, just as the sun had reached its peak. The sun's rays seemed to meet and shine on their charms at a perfect point.

Shamar looked at his dad and said, "Look at your neck, Dad. Look at Mama's too. It's sparkly."

Shamar Sr. smiled and laughed, pulling his baby boy in close to them as they both hugged him.

Moments like this one were the only things his parents had left him with.

Darlene had given the bracelet to Shamar on his fourteenth birthday, the last time they were together. When he saw it, his eyes began to well up. In retrospect, Shamar believed that his mother knew it would probably be the last time they saw each other, and she remembered how much those charms meant to him. The following evening, as he played basketball at a park near his house, his mother was taking her last breath in an overturned car about to go up in flames, and his father was being handcuffed by police.

Not a day went by that he hadn't thought about her and the last day they spent together. She always said she would take care of him and his father, and Shamar knew she meant it, but being alone in the world without them really screwed with his head. It was starting to get to him, and he had to get out of the group home.

"Shamar, didn't I tell you to clean this place up? I don't know why I keep you ungrateful little bastards around. All you do is eat and sleep. Hurry up and get this stuff up before I go upside your head!" Mrs. Turner yelled, interrupting his thoughts.

This was the soundtrack to his life. Every day it seemed it was on repeat, playing at the same time every morning. At 7:30 a.m. promptly, Mrs. Turner marched up and down the hallways, barking orders like a drill sergeant.

I swear she needs to shut up, Joe. It's every day with her, the same thing. You ain't doing this . . . you need to do that. I'm too old for this here, he thought.

Shamar poked his head out of his room, hoping today he'd catch Mrs. Turner in a good mood. He had something important to ask her. As she made her way down the narrow hall, she neared his doorway. With his nerves and stomach tied in knots, he took a deep breath and spoke up to get her attention. "Um . . . Mrs. Turner, I got a question for you," he said.

The obnoxious clunking of her heels on the hardwood floors came to a halt. Mrs. Turner stood with one hand on her hip, and the other held a cigarette to her lips, which were painted with bright red lipstick. "What do you need, boy?" she snapped.

Shamar hesitated at first but quickly shook off the nervousness and answered, "When am I getting out of here? I mean, I'm getting a little too old to be hanging around here, don't you think?" As soon as those words left his lips, he regretted asking. However, now was as good a time as any. He had to know something, and this wasn't the first time he had questioned her.

"Shamar, I told you to stay out of my business, didn't I? Don't worry about getting out of here. I'm the one who's taking care of you. You'll leave here when I say you can leave. Now get that room cleaned!" she said, lightweight scolding him before storming off.

Shamar knew something was off about her. He had been with her in the home for four years now, and at almost eighteen he was beginning to feel like she didn't want him to leave at all. He knew she couldn't keep him there forever, but until he had some kind of paperwork showing it, he was stuck and he felt helpless.

Mrs. Turner was a fifty-year-old widow and unbeknownst to Shamar she had been trying to find every reason she could to keep Shamar around. He was more like her prized possession, and as much as she acted like she despised teenagers, her infatuation with him went beyond the normal bounds of guardianship.

For a woman her age, she was actually quite stunning. Shamar knew she was a widow, but besides the fact that she was so aggressive he couldn't help but wonder why she was still single. He wasn't much into cougars, but it was obvious she was a bad one in her younger days.

When he noticed her getting ready to go out one Friday night, her five foot three frame fit snug as hell inside her jeans, enough to make any young dude get hard. Her thick hips and perky breasts caught his attention every time she pranced around in her house coat. Regardless of what he thought about her physically, Shamar still had a disdain for her because she was the only thing that stood between him and his freedom.

It had been nearly two months since Shamar had last inquired about his being able to leave the group home. One day as he sat in his room he stared out of the window admiring the Chicago skyline. He had his notebook in front of him, which he always kept close to write in as a way of controlling his temper. He imagined he was writing to his mother.

Shamar was only two weeks away from what he believed would be his last day there and he had waited four years for this day to come. Mrs. Turner hadn't given him any information about his ability to leave but, by this point, he had already made up his mind. It would be his eighteenth birthday, and he was going to leave whether she liked it or not. He wanted out, and there was nothing she could do to stop him. In his mind, Shamar decided either she was going to let him leave, or he was going to make her put him out. Legally she could only keep him until his twenty-first birthday, but she made sure not to disclose that information to him.

Mrs. Turner insisted she was only trying to protect Shamar from the streets and it did not help matters when he got locked up a couple summers before for fighting with a cop. Thanks to that and Mrs. Turner's connections it was almost guaranteed that his last years as a teenager would be hell.

The noise in the hallway intensified the longer Mrs. Turner continued her rant. Most of her aggression seemed to be directed at Shamar. He constantly found himself at odds with the authorities like her. His cocky attitude, dreads, and excessive tattoos drew much attention. He continued to pen his frustration through random thoughts as he became more irritated by the sound of Mrs. Turner's voice.

People say I'm a firecracker, but that's because I can't stand when niggas test me and question my ability to hold my own. I try to stay away from people because these dickheads in this group home make a nigga like me very irritable. Mrs. Turner, in her constant drunken state and sloppy demeanor, makes her the most disgusting person I have ever known.

Mrs. Turner interrupted his thoughts when she launched a Bible at him, hitting his shoulder. He couldn't believe she had the nerve even to throw a Bible in his direction. He looked at her like she had two heads. "Man, what you do that for? I told you I was gon' clean up. Man, keep messing with me, Joe. I swear to God, I—" Shamar snapped.

He was fully prepared to spaz out, but she interrupted him. "You gonna what? Boy, you ain't gon' do nothing! You need to pick that Bible up and get you some religion instead of sitting around here doing nothing. Pick it up!"

Mrs. Turner hurled threats and insults at Shamar at times, but it was usually when she felt insecure about him asking when he could leave. She didn't think he picked up on it, but he could tell her anxiety was beginning to increase the more he stood up for himself. Shamar finally conceded and picked up the Bible, throwing it on the bed in an effort to get her to shut up.

As she stormed off, he leaned his chair back against the wall and scribbled on his pad.

I feel like I've been here so long I don't even know what the world is like outside of this place. I go away in my mind when I want to leave here. From here I only wonder what it's really like to actually be able to go somewhere beyond Chicago and, Mama, you always promised you would take me somewhere special one day, but those promises are long gone along with you. Joe, I swear if this old ho don't stop talking to me I'm going to throw this book at her head.

With Mrs. Turner still outside his room, Shamar could hear her stilettos pacing back up the hallway. The smell of her perfume invaded the room, and a cloud of cigarette smoke hovered underneath the light in the middle of the ceiling.

As much as he wanted to pop off again, he knew it would only take one more screwup for her to convince his social worker to extend his stay another six months or more and he was not about to let that happen. The truth was that Mrs. Turner was trying to manipulate him to get a reaction. To her disappointment, he had just sat there staring at her with a grim look on his face hoping that her rant would be over soon. By now he was so stressed that the blunt he had stashed inside the front pocket of his hoodie was starting to call his name.

After another couple of minutes, Mrs. Turner finally felt that she had gotten her point across and she headed down the hall to continue her morning room inspections. *Two more weeks, just two more weeks,* he kept repeating to himself.

Five years later

The word had gotten out that Shamar was on his way back from Arkansas with what was going to be the last pack he would ever move. For three years after leaving the group home, he had gone undetected by the local law enforcement. Now it was time for him to get out of the game, and out of the Midwest, before his luck ran out. Shamar Jackson was a neighborhood hothead with an infatuation for firearms. He found himself living in a small city in Indiana after bouncing around for a couple years. He only ran with two people in the town of Michigan City, Kaduwey and Dee Block, and if anyone ever said anything sideways about either of them in his presence, it was on sight with him.

It was just after midnight on the Friday before Labor Day, the last pack was dropped off, and it was an all-out celebration in honor of Shamar leaving Indiana for good. Through some slick talking and calling in a few favors Shamar found himself enlisting in the Army. It was his only way out of a bad situation. The streets were starting to heat up, and too many people knew his name. It was only a matter of time before the law caught up with him.

His baby's mother, Jelisa, was still trying to wrap her mind around not being able to see him for the next couple of months. As they sat cuddled up in the passenger's seat of his Chevy Caprice, a couple of jump-out boys from South Bend stood in the midst of the crowd as everybody made their way out of the venue to the parking lot. Shamar knew something was off by the look on the two guys' faces. With his arm wrapped around Jelisa's waist, Shamar tapped her on her leg, signaling for her to get up.

"Hey, go over there with Ashley for a minute. I need to handle something real quick," he said, trying not to raise concern. She did as he said and, like clockwork, Block and Kaduwey both emerged from behind Shamar's car and stood on both sides of him as he stood up. "Y'all see what I see?" Shamar asked.

"Yo, keep it cool, G. We ain't here for all that," Kaduwey said, noticing Shamar's hand slowly moving toward the strap he had tucked under his hoodie.

"Yeah, dawg, don't do nothing stupid. There's too many people here," Block agreed. They both knew that once Shamar locked in on somebody, there wasn't much anyone could say to talk him down.

"Ay, fam, what the hell is you staring at? You got a problem or something?" Shamar questioned.

The two goons continued ice grilling them as one reached for his waist. Without hesitation, Shamar pulled out and started busting in their direction. The crowd scrambled as the sounds of women screaming and tires screeching filled the air. The would-be robbers returned fire as Shamar and his crew ducked behind his car.

"G, I told you to cool out. What the hell are you doing?" Kaduwey yelled while also returning fire.

"What you mean? You see they bussin' at us too. Just be glad I got the drop on them," Shamar answered.

The two jump-out boys took off, darting across the lot and disappearing into the crowd. As the crowd dispersed, police sirens were heard in the distance. The three friends jumped in Shamar's car and followed suit, seeing that their girlfriends were already gone. They drove down Washington Street and made the first turn available, heading toward the west side, in the opposite direction of everyone else.

Once they got to Block's spot and the coast was clear, the fellas sat in the basement and shared a laughed.

Block commented, "G, you wild, boy. I'm telling you. How are you leaving tomorrow and you shooting up the spot tonight? That don't make sense. You must really want to go out with a bang."

Shamar grinned and nodded in agreement. "Yeah, it's definitely time for me to get out of here. I'm gonna mess around and catch a case real quick," he said.

"Well, G, it's been real, homie. Just make sure you don't come back here all shell-shocked.

Then we really won't be able to do nothing with you," Kaduwey added.

Shamar went to the bar and poured three shots of Hennessy. They stood and raised their glasses and toasted one last time. Shamar spoke, saying, "Y'all my Day Ones. It's all love to my death!"

Chapter One

Jelisa couldn't believe Shamar had to go back overseas so soon. He had just come back from Germany, where he had been stationed for two years. She couldn't come with him because they hadn't gotten married yet. They had just eloped on Christmas Eve while Shamar was in the process of moving back stateside. Jelisa had had her fill of the long flights every few months to go visit him in Germany. She was led to believe that after they married she would be able to go anywhere he went.

It was now March and after having only been back in the States for a few short months Shamar's new unit was already preparing to send him off to join the rest of his company, who were already deployed. Knowing that he was newly married, his unit gave him some extra time to get prepared to go. On this day, his unit was due to leave Fort Riley, Kansas, for Iraq in less than two hours and tensions were high.

Shamar did his best to keep his composure in an effort to keep Jelisa calm, but deep inside he was terrified. It seemed that their three-year-old daughter, Mya, was the only one who picked up on it.

"Jelisa, don't do this to me now; I told you I'm good. It's nothing to be scared of. I'm not even going to be on the front lines; remember, I'm a medic. I'll be all the way in the back," Shamar said. His six foot two inch frame towered over her, as she stood only five feet four inches. With one arm wrapped around her shoulder and the other holding Mya, he tried to make the most of these final moments.

"Whatever, Shamar, stop telling me that. You don't know what's going to happen," Jelisa countered, rolling her eyes. "What are we supposed to do while you're gone? I'm not staying in Kansas by myself; I don't know nobody besides the people you've introduced me to from your unit. I want to be with my own family while you're gone," Jelisa pleaded.

She was nineteen with a pretty face and a smart mouth. Her silky hair rested on her shoulders, and her brown skin glowed in the sunlight. However, it was her smart mouth that Shamar was drawn to; at the same time, it was also the one thing that irked him the most about her. She didn't seem to know when to shut up.

"Are you done yet?" he asked with a dead stare on his face. "You're not making this easy for me; you know that, right?" Shamar hated when she laid guilt trips on him, but he understood she was scared something would happen to him. He made her promise never to watch the news. The media never portrayed the good things the soldiers were doing, and he didn't want her freaking out. "Listen, I promise you that I'm going to do everything I can to make it back here. This year is going to go by fast, okay? I told you that you don't have to stay here if you don't want to. If you don't want to come back here after you go and see your mom, by all means, stay up there until I get back. I just want y'all to be looked after," he explained.

He caressed her cheek and kissed her, hoping to give her some comfort. In her mind, she felt like it would be the last kiss, like he was abandoning her. But what was he supposed to do? It was his job.

"Sergeant Jackson, we need to get everybody formed up!" another sergeant shouted from across the way.

Shamar looked over at the sergeant, nodding his head in acknowledgement, and then he looked back at Jelisa. With the most sincerity she had seen in his eyes since Mya was born, he asked, "You love me?" as he pulled her in closer to him.

"Yeah, Shamar, you know I do," she responded as a tear formed at the corner of her eye.

"All right, then trust me. I love you too. Now let me get over here. Mya, Daddy loves you, okay?" Shamar kissed his daughter on the cheek and put her down. He gave Jelisa one last hug before grabbing his bags and walking away. Shamar headed to an awaiting bus that was to take him and the other soldiers to the municipal airport. This would be the first in a series of flights taking them to their final destination in Iraq.

Jelisa watched in anguish, thinking, *What am I going to do without him? What if he doesn't come back? God, why is this happening now?*

Thoughts of all of the talks they had about traveling the world, and giving Mya the life they never had, began to race through her mind, filling her with anxiety. Tears began to race down her cheeks as she held Mya tight making sure that she got one last glimpse of her father.

As he stared out of the window from his seat, Shamar fought back tears as well as the urge to get back off of the bus and run to his wife and child. He had no idea it would be this difficult to leave them.

As the bus began to pull off, Shamar and Jelisa locked eyes one last time. Shamar mouthed the words, "I love you," holding his gaze until she and Mya were no longer in sight.

After taking several deep breaths, Jelisa accepted he was gone, then turned and walked away. She and Mya then got into an awaiting cab and left, heading back to their hotel. They went back to the Holiday Inn, where they had been staying, to finish packing up their things so they could go back to Indiana. Shamar would be gone for a year, and Jelisa began to wonder if they should have waited to get married.

They weren't high school sweethearts or anything; in fact, they had never dated before she got pregnant. Their beautiful little princess, Mya, was the result of a one-night stand after a house party when Jelisa was sixteen. Shamar was nineteen at the time, so it took two years of them dealing with each other for him to even start considering making her his main chick. After considering the thought of another man being in his daughter's life, he made his mind up to be there one way or another.

Jelisa didn't know the first thing about being a wife; but if it meant she and her baby girl would be taken care of, she was with it. Now with this deployment at hand, she would have to go another twelve months without seeing him. The uncertainty of the days to come terrified her.

When their plane landed at O'Hare Airport, Jelisa and Mya took a bus from Chicago to Michigan City. When they arrived at the drop-off point, her mother, Sandra, was waiting for them. Her beat-up 1984 Chevy Caprice was a stark reminder of what she was trying to escape when she chose to leave with Shamar. The members of the Adams family not only shared the same name, but they also shared the same mentality of holding on to things for as long as possible. In other words, being broke was a family tradition, and it was one Jelisa had no intention of passing down.

Oh my God, no, she did not come and pick me up in this car, she thought as she struggled to drag her luggage in one hand with Mya trailing slowly behind her, holding the other.

"Hey, honey, how was your flight?" Sandra said, going straight to Mya. "Come here, Granny's baby, give me some kisses." Mya quickly let go of Jelisa's hand and ran into her grandmother's arms.

"Hey, Mama, it was okay. You know I hate traveling with her by myself. Ugh," Jelisa grunted in frustration.

"Well, baby, that's part of being a mother. I can't say I feel bad for you. Y'all go on and get in so we can get back to the house. I left my oven on."

Jelisa sucked her teeth and threw her luggage in the back seat. She buckled Mya into her car seat before painstakingly getting into the front passenger's seat. As they merged onto the main road, Jelisa sat silently, staring out the window.

"Child, what's wrong with you? You're not worried about Shamar, are you?" Sandra asked, already knowing the answer to her question.

"Mama, I don't know how to feel about it. I mean, he told me not to worry; but what if something does happen to him?"

Sandra wasn't convinced that this was the only thing she was concerned about. "Girl, please, the Army ain't no different than these streets out here. You didn't have any problems when Shamar was out here selling dope and having shootouts every other week. What's really going on with you?"

Jelisa wasn't expecting that, but Sandra never held any punches when it came to her daughter. She was the youngest, so she always required more from her than her sisters did.

"Jelisa! Jelisa, are you listening to me?"

She wasn't ignoring her. As she stared off, she was thinking back to times when she sat up at night, calling around, trying to find Shamar after hearing that he'd been involved in something. She finally snapped out of it and looked over, cutting her eyes at Sandra. "Mama, you don't know what you talkin' about. You always in somebody's business. You weren't there when I sat up worrying about the shootouts and fights. The Army was supposed to take us away from stuff like this, but it seems like he just left one war to go fight another one. Who's supposed to take care of us? Huh?" she snapped. Jelisa wasn't feeling this whole situation, and she couldn't wait until they got home so she could get out of the car.

"Look, I know you're scared of losing him, but you have to take the good with the bad. You just make sure you do right by him while he's away. You know what I'm talking about?"

Jelisa leaned away from her and frowned, slightly offended by the suggestion that she might cheat on Shamar. "Excuse me? What you mean by that?" she asked.

She knew exactly what her mother was talking about, but she hadn't messed around on Shamar since they got married, and the time she did step out no one ever knew about. That was something she intended to leave in the past. "Mama, please leave me alone, because you don't know what you talkin' 'bout. I wish you would mind your own business. I'm not going to be staying with you for long; I know that much. I can't deal with this for a whole year. God!"

Jelisa was tight now; she really hated when Sandra pried into her business. Her stay with her mother would only be temporary. Shamar told her to find an apartment as soon as she could. "Mama, can you please just let it go? And why are you taking the long way? We should've been on the east side by now," Jelisa snapped, noticing that Sandra had passed their turn, and she hadn't mentioned needing to go anywhere else along the way.

"Your father called and asked me to bring you and Mya by so he could see y'all." Unlike most girls she knew, Jelisa actually knew her father and had a decent relationship with him; but what she loved about him the most was the fact that he always took her side. He and her mother had been divorced since she was twelve years old. When he found out she was pregnant, he was the only one who didn't flip out on her.

"All right. I wonder why he didn't call me. Hmm. Mya, you wanna go see Papa?" she looked back and asked. Jelisa was grateful for her father, Pete. He was considered the cool parent.

When they pulled up to Pete's house, he was sitting on the porch, smoking his pipe. He waved as they parked. As soon as Jelisa opened the door and unbuckled Mya, she bolted and headed straight for him. "Papa!" she yelled with the biggest smile on her face.

"Hey, baby, come and give me a hug." His raspy voice was a result of how sick he had been lately, but Pete Adams would have no one feeling sorry for him.

"Hey, Daddy, how you doing?"

Pete let out a gut-wrenching cough. "Aw, baby, I'm still breathing. How was the trip?"

Jelisa just knew he was going to have something to say about her relationship sooner or later. Pete was just like any other concerned father, and even though he usually stayed out of her business, for some reason she knew it was coming. "It was fine, Daddy. But, seriously, are you doing all right?" Her concern for his health was growing more every time she saw him.

Pete skated past her question and turned his attention to Sandra. "Sandra, how you holding up? You sounded a little stressed on the phone."

Jelisa rolled her eyes and let out a deep sigh. She hated when he did that.

"Pete, what I'm dealing with is none of your concern," Sandra said sternly. In her eyes, he no longer had the right to question her about anything that didn't involve the kids or grandkids. "By the sound of it, you're the one who needs to be looked after," she added.

Pete leaned up, adjusted himself, and let out another harsh cough. "Well, maybe you should do something about that," he said jokingly. He loved getting under her skin.

"Old man, you better go on somewhere; ain't nobody got time to be messing with you," Sandra retorted.

While they went back and forth, picking on each other, Jelisa picked Mya up, sat her on Pete's knee, and walked back to the sidewalk. She gazed up at the sky, watching as it grew darker by the minute. Her parents' breakup was the reason she was hesitant when it came to getting married. Pete and Sandra were once the best of friends; so if they didn't work out, Jelisa wondered if there was even any hope for her and Shamar.

Twenty minutes passed, and they were still talking. Growing impatient, Jelisa walked up and interrupted, "Okay, Daddy, we need to get out of here. I have to feed Mya, and I'm hungry myself."

Pete nodded his head. He knew she wouldn't wait much longer. "All right, well, you all stop by and see me this week. I'm thinking about having a barbeque. Oh, yeah, before I forget, how you doing now that your husband is gone? You gonna be all right?"

She hated when he asked about her love life. She knew no matter what she would eventually find herself having to defend whatever her latest decisions were. At this point, Pete was probably the only person who could get away with asking.

"Daddy, I'm okay. I just need to get used to him not being around. I'm good, I promise."

He smirked and raised his hands in submission, not wanting to push the issue. After a few more minutes, the ladies were ready to go. Pete hugged all three of them and watched from the sidewalk as they returned to the car and drove away. If only he could be closer. He knew Jelisa was going to have a hard time getting used to being alone, but there was nothing he could do. At least when Shamar was in Germany, she was able to see him every couple of months. However, this situation was different, seeing as how it would be nothing but phone calls and letters for the whole year.

Chapter Two

Shamar

Three hours after he and Jelisa left the airfield, Shamar was on a plane headed for Kuwait. The next day, after being briefed, his unit was staged in Baghdad, waiting to convoy up to northern Iraq. He sat next to his friend Omar, whom he'd known since basic training.

Omar was a reformed ladies' man, and this was his second time going to Iraq; the first deployment he went on nearly destroyed his marriage. There was an issue of infidelity on both his and his wife's parts. The stress of being away from his family and his wife, not knowing if she would get that dreadful call about him being killed, was enough to drive a wedge between them. Omar's marriage was in complete shambles by the time he made it back home. It took a toll on them both, but they managed to repair the damage that was done from her cheating back home and him trying to fill a void while deployed. This time around, he felt even worse knowing that his wife, Kyana, would be on her own doing God knows what.

"Bruh, I hope this broad don't act up while I'm gone. I'm telling you, I swear I'ma kill somebody if she try me," Omar said, pounding his fist into his hand.

"Man, be easy, bruh. She ain't stupid. Y'all good. You got a rider, man. Everybody makes mistakes. You just gotta trust that she learned her lesson or take it as a loss and move on."

Omar nodded, knowing Shamar was making sense. Shamar tried to identify with him, but it was hard because, being a player himself, he expected women to cheat; he just didn't want to find out about it. This mindset served him well, only because he could never prove Jelisa ever did. Being in the streets taught him not to put trust in too many people, but it was different with her because she was the mother of his child.

"See, man, you ain't trippin' 'cause you know Jelisa ain't dumb enough to step out on you. I don't wanna jinx you or anything, but this is her first deployment so ain't no telling how she gon' act, feel me?"

Shamar didn't want to admit it, but Omar was right. It never was an issue with them. During the times when they were just messing around, whenever he came back into the picture Jelisa cut off everybody else she had been dealing with to be with him. "Yeah, I feel you. I'm just saying you gotta give her the benefit of trusting she won't act up. That's all I'm saying."

A voice over the intercom informed them that they had hit their cruising altitude, so Omar leaned his seat back and tried to get some sleep. It would be another seven hours before they reached the first stop.

Shamar also tried sleeping, but he was having a hard time because something didn't feel right. He was usually on to something when that feeling came over him. He started thinking about the argument he had with Jelisa the week before. As he replayed each moment of it, what Omar said made more sense.

Shamar had been home for a few days on leave to spend some time with the family before he left. While they were sitting in the living room at Sandra's house, she asked him if he wanted any more kids. "Yeah, I don't know about that," he said, raising his eyebrows and looking up at the ceiling.

"Why you say that?" she asked.

Jelisa looked over at her and said, "Mama, please don't. I'm really not trying to get into this right now. I don't know if I want any more kids, at least not right now."

Shamar put his head down and started playing with his cell phone, knowing he didn't want to be part of the conversation anymore.

"Child, please," Sandra said, blowing Jelisa off. "You better give this man some kids. Shamar, how do you feel about it?"

He hesitated to respond but, by now, both of them were staring at him, waiting for an answer. Jelisa had this look on her face that said, "You better not."

But unwilling to be challenged, Shamar spoke up. "Like I said before, it's her body. I'm not the one who has to carry a baby; so, if she ain't ready, it's whatever. I do want a few more kids, though, but I'm not going to make her do something she don't want to do."

Jelisa rolled her eyes and let out a deep sigh. She knew Sandra wasn't going to let that one go, but she had her reasons for not wanting any more kids.

"Now, Jelisa, I'm not trying to get in your business, but you need to give that man some kids before one of these other heifers out here tries to. You got yourself a good man here who actually has something going for himself. Don't be stupid."

Jelisa looked at Shamar with disgust and mumbled under her breath, "Why you have to say something?"

One thing he hated was being heckled by a woman, so that was enough to push him. He snapped back, "Jelisa, don't play with me! Don't think because your mom is sitting here I won't snatch you up. Who you think you talking to?"

Sandra just sat back and nodded in agreement. She had always told her daughter never to disrespect a man's ego. She wasn't going to let him put his hands on her, but Jelisa needed a reality check. She knew her daughter was selfish.

"Ugh, you get on my nerves!" she shouted, storming out of the living room into the kitchen. Shamar jumped up and followed right behind her, cornering her by the sink. She tried pushing her way past him. "Move, Shamar! Get out of my way!"

He pushed her back and palmed her chin, controlling her movement. "Jelisa, what the hell is your problem? Don't you ever talk to me like that, especially in front of yo' mama."

She snatched away, folded her arms, and rolled her eyes.

"Look, shawty, don't play with me. You know I got you, and you know I don't care about

*having no kids right now, but you need to
understand that it's going to have to happen
eventually. You just need to stop being so extra
right now. I don't appreciate that at all."*

Jelisa didn't respond; she just looked away.

"Look at me. You love me?"

She whispered under her breath, "Yeah."

*Shamar reached out, pulled her close to him,
hugged her, and kissed her on her forehead.*

*They walked back into the living room and
sat down. Sandra had a satisfied look on her
face. As much as she questioned their relationship at times, she knew that there was
something about the two of them together that
worked.*

*Shamar never stopped thinking about that
incident. Since he wasn't the type to fight about
stuff, he didn't bring it up. In addition, with the
deployment coming up, he didn't want to leave
on a sour note.*

The plane hit some turbulence, which snapped
him out of his daydream. He looked over at
Omar and nudged his arm. "Hey, bruh, you
think she gon' be cool while I'm gone?"

Omar shrugged his shoulders and lifted his
eyebrows. "I don't know, man. You know her
better than I do. You tell me."

It was finally starting to hit him. What if Jelisa did do something stupid? He had seen a lot of soldiers' wives creep on them while they were deployed, but he always thought Jelisa was too smart for that because she had everything she needed. He never put anything past her, though. He always suspected she had stepped out. No woman was that loyal. But since he couldn't prove it, he let it go. Being around so many people having issues with their marriages made Shamar reconsider his views on a woman's ability to be faithful.

"Dawg, don't let that stuff get to you. She'll be straight. Just make sure you keep in touch with her so she never feels like you're unreachable, feel me?"

Shamar nodded his head in agreement. He didn't like feeling vulnerable, but most dudes he knew got that way when it came to the mothers of their children. Things were starting to seem more realistic the more he thought about the kinds of temptations Jelisa might have to face in his absence. "Yeah, you right. I'm trippin'. This stuff is stressing me out, man. I just don't want any surprises, feel me?"

***

It didn't take long for the word to get out that Jelisa would be coming back to the city. She wasn't at all worried about what people would think about it because it would only be temporary, assuming they made it through this deployment. There was one person who took this time as an opportunity to finally get what he wanted: Donny, the owner of the Platinum Designs Barber Shop and Salon, where Jelisa used to work on the west side. He was a very calculated person; everything he did had its purpose. He didn't believe in coincidences. He was able to adjust to any situation. He didn't think twice about offering her a chair when she asked to come back.

The previous week, Donny had overheard Lanette, one of his stylists, talking to a customer. The shop was busy, and the smell of hot irons and oil sheen filled the air. With music playing in the background, it was buzzing, even for a Monday.

"Girl, you know Shamar is going to be gone for a whole year, right? I don't know how Jelisa gon' do it," the customer said, smacking her lips and shaking her head.

Lanette hated to be in the middle of a mess, and she didn't have anything against Jelisa. She replied, "Girl, that's they business. I don't have nothing to do with that. He's taking care of her anyway, so I don't see what's so hard about it. All she gotta do is wait for him to come home." That was simple enough for her; it didn't call for all the extra stuff, and she wasn't going to add to it.

As they continued to talk, Donny continued to listen and started to plot how he was going to conquer Jelisa. She had shut him down so many times and stated on more than one occasion that Shamar was all the man she needed. Donny knew him from the streets, so he wasn't too convinced that she actually knew who he really was. He wasn't trying to rat him out, but he was so tired of hearing everyone say how good Shamar was to her. Donny was determined to knock her down one good time to prove she wasn't as committed as she thought she was. To him, women were only prizes that went to the most cunning and skilled players; there was no room for emotions. Something he often said to himself was, "Emotions will get you killed." So if it was true that he would have Jelisa all to himself for a year, he was going to take her for all she had and make her feel good about it.

That Monday morning after dropping Mya off at daycare, Jelisa headed back to work.

She had been planning for a week to come back after helping Shamar prepare to leave and packing up his stuff to go into storage. It was chilly outside; this wasn't the type of Monday she was particularly fond of. The fall weather brought a sort of depressing mood to the morning. Jelisa woke up with an attitude, so having to go into work on a Monday when all of the other shops in town were closed irritated her. But Donny was also a hustler, so it made sense to him to be the only shop open, and it worked.

The cool air stalked her as she walked from her car to the front door of the shop. She hoped that Donny was already there, as it would save her the trouble of fumbling with her keys in the cold. Sure enough, there he was standing with his back turned toward the door with Meek Mill playing loud on the stereo. As she walked through the door, he didn't even notice that she was standing behind him. She found herself admiring him as he danced from side to side until he noticed her in the mirror.

"Hey, what's good, baby girl? When did you get back?"

His grin coupled with his Polo cologne caught her off guard. She got chills out of nowhere, but she caught herself and shook it off.

"Hey, Donny, what's up? Yeah, I got back yesterday. What's going on for today?" she asked, walking into the back room to put her coat and bag away. As she bent over, tucking her bag in the corner of the room, Donny stood in the doorway with his head tilted sideways. She could feel him standing behind her, so she peeked over her shoulder and smiled. "What you looking at? Boy, you better go somewhere." Jelisa thought it was cute how he often checked her out. She would sometimes flirt back with him, but she always made sure he knew where to draw the line. Donny stood five feet eleven inches with dark chocolate skin and 360-degree waves that perfectly circled his head. His chiseled chest flexed as he went back to sweeping. Jelisa again found herself admiring his athletic build, which was somewhat hidden behind his white tee.

"So soldier boy's gone, huh? What you got planned to do with your time now that you don't have anyone to spend it with?" Donny asked, toying with her as he turned down the music.

"I've got enough on my plate with my daughter. I don't have time for nothing else. Why you so concerned about what I'm doing anyway? Don't you have a woman?" She knew where he was going with his line of questions; but the sting of Shamar being gone was still fresh, so Donny didn't stand a chance.

What she didn't know was that Donny was a patient predator. Having been around the military lifestyle before, he knew it was only a matter of time before the distance would be too much for her. When that time came, he'd be more than ready for it. "Aww, baby girl, you know I'm just messing with you. Why you always gotta bring my ol' lady into it? I thought we were better than that."

Jelisa was no longer amused. She was more concerned about how long it would take for her to hear from Shamar. Just as she thought about it, her phone rang. But it wasn't him; it was her mother, Sandra. Disappointed, she slowly pressed TALK and answered the phone. "Yes, Mama, what's wrong?" she said, thinking Sandra was being her typical nosy self.

"Jelisa, you better lose that attitude, little girl. So, listen here, I need you to help me with something."

Jelisa grew a disgusted look on her face as she anticipated what her mother's next words would be. Whenever Sandra wanted to borrow some money, she would start the conversation with "So, listen here."

"What, Mama? How much do you need? Ugh!"

Sandra could hear the attitude in her voice, but she had no problem asking for what she needed. "Look, I need some help with the gas bill. I only have a few dollars. Can you take care of it for me?"

This was one of the reasons Jelisa didn't want to stay at home with her. She knew that the family would try to take advantage of her getting Shamar's military pay. Sandra would never admit it, but she actually felt like Jelisa owed her after all of the sacrifices she had made raising her. Not wanting to talk in front of Donny, Jelisa went into the back room and grabbed her purse and jacket. "Donny, I gotta make this run real quick. I have an appointment at eleven, but I'll be back before then. You need me to pick up anything?"

He shook his head no and watched as she prepared herself to go out. She walked to the car, regretting she even answered the phone.

As she started it up and headed down the road, Sandra began to explain why she needed the money so badly. "Look, you know I don't even like asking you for money but I really need this. I promise I'll pay you back."

Jelisa took the phone away from her ear and looked at it in disbelief. "Mama, stop making promises you know you can't keep. If you were able to pay me back, you wouldn't be asking for it in the first place. Now, I gave you eight hundred dollars before I left to go see Shamar off. What did you spend that money on?"

Sandra got quiet; that was an indication that something else was up.

"Mama, don't play with me. I can't keep giving you money every time you ask for it. You gotta—"

Sandra interrupted her, "You really gon' do this to me after all I've done for you? Watching your child, picking her up and dropping her off. So what I ask you for some money every now and then? Hell, it's the least you can do since your father . . ." She caught herself and let out a sigh.

"Since Daddy what, Mama? Why do you always have to bring him up whenever we get into it? You were the one who caused problems between y'all, not me." Jelisa was a few minutes from the house when she decided to bypass it and drive out to Pete's.

"Jelisa, just forget about it! Never mind, I'll figure something out. Keep your money." Sandra was like a highly trained FBI agent; she had an awesome ability to manipulate people into doing what she wanted. But Jelisa was genuinely shaken up by the argument. She always felt like Sandra hated her and treated her worse than anyone else because she reminded her so much of Pete. She loved her mother; but, too often, doing things for her put her at odds with Shamar. He told her all the time not to let her family use her; but with him being gone, her family was all she had.

"Mama, whatever, I'll see you when I get home. I can't do this right now. Good-bye!" She quickly hung up before Sandra could get another word out. "I can't stand when she does that. God!" she said out loud. The guilt trip Sandra had just laid on her brought her to tears and left her torn between helping her mother and respecting Shamar's instructions to not let herself be used. "How am I going to explain this to Shamar? He is going to have a whole fit."

A few minutes later, she pulled up to Pete's house. As usual, he was sitting on the porch smoking his pipe. Jelisa took a couple of seconds to gather herself. As she walked up the sidewalk, Pete straightened himself up in his chair. Seeing her put a huge smile on his face. "Hey, baby, what's going on with you? What's the matter? You look like you've been crying."

As much as she tried to disguise it, he saw right through her. "Nothing, Daddy. Me and Mama got into it again. You know how that goes."

Pete nodded his head and motioned for her to come onto the porch. "I know what you mean, honey. Well, your mother is a different kind of woman. She is still hurt by the things I did and how I left. Go on and have a seat." The air was cool and gentle. The morning sun beamed on her just enough to keep her warm. "You know, your mother and I tried to shield you and your sisters from the drama we had going on. Raising four girls wasn't the easiest thing for me, and I know I wasn't the best example." His eyes started welling up as he continued. Jelisa didn't know if he was about to cry or if the wind blowing was causing it. "I put your mother through hell; and with you being strong-willed like me, I knew she was taking her hatred of me out on you."

Jelisa could hardly remember her childhood but what she did remember still carried a sting with it. "Daddy, I know you guys thought we didn't know what was going on, but we did. I just hate that she blames me for you leaving."

Pete took another puff from his pipe and let out a harsh cough. "There's a lot you don't know, and it's not really my place to tell you. But I will say this: my mistress was the one thing that ruined our marriage. I couldn't think straight whenever she was in the picture. I know that you girls didn't deserve that, and I wish to God I could take it back."

She hated when he used the term "mistress" because it wasn't another woman he was referring to. He was talking about his heroin addiction. Pete didn't like to admit that he had a drug problem. It was more comforting for him to say he had some commitment issues.

"Daddy, I just feel like she's using me. It's hard enough trying to cope with Shamar being gone, but to have to put up with this is too much. I'm going to have to get my own place; and even with that, I know she's going to try to stop me because she won't be able to say I owe anything."

Pete cleared his throat and turned and grabbed her hand. "Look at me, Jelisa. You have to do what's best for you and your family. Now, there is a reason why I didn't have a problem with you marrying Shamar. I know he comes from a good family. His dad and I used to be neighbors, and I got drafted with his uncle. Now, don't you let your mother convince you to do anything that will disrespect your husband. That's one concept she never understood. She let your grandmother push her to do and say things no woman should ever do or say to her husband. So you go get your own place, and you do right by that man and support him while he's gone. He needs you more than you think. You hear me?"

She contemplated what he was saying and she was grateful that he had taken the time to talk with her honestly. But time was getting away from her, and it was close to 10:30, so she needed to head back to the shop. "All right, Daddy. Well, I love you and thank you so much for listening. I appreciate it. I'm going to do what you said. Pray for me. I have to get back to the shop." They both stood up and hugged each other and Pete walked her to her car.

As she drove off, he hoped she would really take heed of his words. He knew she was just as stubborn as he was and sometimes had to learn things the hard way. For now, there was nothing he could do but pray. He went and sat back on the porch and hoped everything would get better for her.

Chapter Three

Block

Life for Block was just as rocky as it was for Shamar, even though they grew up in different cities. While one of his best friends was on the other side of the world fighting in a war, Block, whose real name was Darron Foster, was just coming home after losing a war with the judicial system.

It was the middle of the day about six months before Shamar had headed to basic training. Thirty-three-year-old Darron sat on a bench in the Indiana state prison courtyard, watching as the cars passed. The streets they rode down were the same ones he used to run when he was a teen in the late eighties. He was three days from being released after serving half of a thirty-year bid for manslaughter. The bright sun beat down on his broad shoulders as he sat with his back turned away from the rest of the population, the reason being he didn't want any of the other inmates to see the anxiety that covered his face. It was the same look he displayed in the municipal courtroom fifteen years ago as the prosecutor gave an account of the events that put him there.

District Prosecuting Attorney Michael Hanson stood before the court, facing the jury and holding a sawed-off shotgun. Darron sat with a dead stare that intimidated every juror in the room, dressed in a black tailored three-piece suit, his hair pulled back into a bushy ponytail with a razor sharp line that outlined his thin beard. His dark chocolate skin was smooth and flawless, and there was nothing about this young man that fit the stereotypical description of a killer. His friends and family knew him as Dee Block or Dark Block, a nickname he had picked up one summer after visiting family in California. He had never been exposed to so much sun before, and when he returned to Indiana, he was the darkest anyone had ever seen him. The eighteen-year-old high school student was mere months from graduating when he found himself caught in the middle of an argument between his sister and her boyfriend.

Attorney Hanson spoke loud with conviction, trying to appease the audience. The jury of middle-aged white men and women who were sup-

posed to be a jury of his peers sat with their minds already made up. "Ladies and gentlemen of the jury, I'll ask that you would close your eyes and go back with me to the night in question. After a night of partying, drinking, and smoking, the deceased Joshua Townsend and his long-time girlfriend, Latoya Foster, got into an argument over a rumor that he had cheated on her," he said.

This theatrical performance the DA was putting on could have won him an Oscar. The jury was putty in his hands. He continued, as he paced across the room, "Imagine this young man Joshua, an all-star high school football player, is your son. He and Ms. Foster are going back and forth, yelling and screaming accusations, and suddenly things get out of hand. Young Joshua, trying to keep Ms. Foster from striking him, accidentally smacks her in the eye, and she falls and hits her head on the corner of a coffee table. She is knocked unconscious, and blood is seen on the floor. Now, Joshua, terribly remorseful, attempts to wake her up by lightly slapping her cheek. In comes the defendant, Mr. Foster, her younger brother, who is twice the size of Joshua. He asks no questions. Instead, he pulls out a sawed-off shotgun from behind the living room couch and shoots Joshua

*in the chest as he turns around to try to explain
what happened. With no concern for the lives of
anyone else in the house, Mr. Foster takes the
life of a young man who was only guilty of acci-
dently hitting his girlfriend."*

*Block was noticeably irritated as he listened
to this DA make a mockery of the court system
with the lies he was spewing to the jury.* Man, I
can't believe he really gonna stand up there and
lie like that.

He reached for a nearby notepad and wrote:

> You know that's not what happened.
> What are we going to do? They are buying
> it.

*He then slid it over to his lawyer, Attorney
Jonathan Bush. He was one of the top African
American defense attorneys in the region.
Block's uncle Alex put up the money for his legal
fees mainly because he believed his nephew
only did it to protect his sister.*

Attorney Bush wrote back on the paper:

> Don't worry, they won't get a murder
> conviction. Too many holes in the story.
> Just calm down. They're watching you.
> Don't feed into it.

***

When the trial first began, Attorney Bush was straightforward with Block. He told him that because of the way LaPorte County was when it came to young African American males he was likely to get some time. However, because he was defending the life of another person, he was sure to beat the murder charge. Although he didn't want to have to become the kind of person it would take to survive in prison, the life of his big sister was worth it. Block showed no remorse for taking one life to save another; he'd do that time proudly.

When it came time for the defense to give its closing arguments Attorney Bush painted a totally different picture. He actually told the truth about what happened. Latoya had been going hard on Joshua because he had been caught cheating with one of her friends. The two twenty-one-year-olds had always had trust issues during their four-year relationship. What the DA didn't mention was the fact that, on multiple occasions before, Joshua had been accused of putting his hands on other females. Because of his status as an athletic star, complaints were usually dropped. This was what led to the confrontation between Block and Joshua. When he came into his mother's house,

Block did not see what the DA called light slaps in an attempt to wake Latoya. What he saw was Joshua pounding away at his sister's lifeless body. The bruises on the photos that had been passed around to the jury earlier were proof of this. Block shooting Joshua was purely to save the life of his sister and after the defense ended its statements, it would be left up to the jury to decide his fate.

The jury came back in less than three hours of deliberating. That alone made Block nervous, but no matter how it went, he stood by his decision, and his sister and the rest of the family were behind him. Beads of sweat rolled down the small of his back, and anxiety painted his face. He had grown several gray hairs in the middle of the head as a result of the stress.

When the verdict was read the entire courtroom was silent. "We, the jury, find the defendant, Darron Foster, not guilty on the count of first-degree murder," one juror read from a sheet of paper.

The room erupted with cheers from the Block family and cries from Joshua's. The judge banged his gavel and demanded to have order in the court. He followed with a statement on behalf of the state of Indiana. "Mr. Foster, you have been found not guilty of murder, but the court still finds you grossly responsible for taking the life of another human being. It is the court's judgment that you are hereby found guilty of voluntary manslaughter in the death of Joshua Townsend. Sentencing will take place in two weeks."

As the judge put the court in recess until sentencing, Block remained standing in disbelief. His heart dropped. Even though he knew going in he would have to do some time, he never expected this charge. At the least, he thought he might get an assault charge just due to the fact that the judge had a point to prove. He leaned over and asked his lawyer, "Can he do that? What just happened?"

Attorney Bush, who was just as frustrated, knew there was a slight chance this could happen; but he'd only seen it once before. "Yes, unfortunately, he can. If the judge finds that the crime qualifies for a lesser charge he can rule in favor of it. Trust me, the DA knew they couldn't get the murder conviction but they also knew he wouldn't just let you walk. We're still going to fight this, son," he said, trying to keep him calm.

Two weeks later the judge handed down a sentence of thirty years with the possibility of parole in fifteen. Block made a promise to his family to do everything he could to come home in fifteen. Being a man of his word, he did exactly that, and now after fifteen long years in a prison twenty minutes from his childhood home, Block was ready to return to society.

These next three days couldn't go by any faster. As the signal sounded for the population to return to the cell blocks, Block caught a glimpse of the roof of his best friend Straw's old house. He hadn't seen him in a couple of years, and word on the tier was that he had left town on the run from the feds. It was a sober moment for him, and just as his mind began to drift off, one of the COs blew a whistle to get his attention. Block returned to his cell and sat quietly as the cell slammed shut.

Chapter Four

Shamar

A week had gone by, and Shamar was finally able to call home. Because of the nature of their mission, he wasn't allowed to mention where he was and there were specific times he was allowed to call. Let him tell it, it was almost like being in jail.

It was a Tuesday evening, and Jelisa had just returned from the grocery store. As she was putting things away, the house phone rang. She looked around with frustration, wondering why nobody else in the house attempted to answer it. Already on edge after having to deal with Mya's whining the whole time they were at the store, she slammed a can of vegetables on the counter and sucked her teeth. She walked back into the living room and grabbed the cordless phone off the charger. Looking at the caller ID, she didn't recognize the Tennessee number, so she was tempted to ignore it. She then remembered that Shamar said that he would have to use calling cards to call out so she should expect calls from out-of-town numbers. Taking the risk of it just being a bill collector or telemarketer, she braced herself and pressed TALK on the phone.

"Hello," she spoke, unenthused.

"Hey, baby girl, what's up? You miss me yet?" Shamar said in his best Barry White impression.

Elated at the sound of his voice, Jelisa's face lit up as her heart fluttered with excitement. She was beginning to wonder if she'd ever hear from him. She was worried that something might have happened to him. "Hey, babe, yeah, I miss you. Why did it take so long for you to call me? You got me over here freaking out," she said.

He could hear the sincerity in her voice, so he attempted to reassure her that he was okay. "I know, I know. It's kind of crazy over here. I've just been trying to get things in order. But I'm good. Can't wait to see you again. How have you been holding up?"

His attempts, however ineffective, didn't go unnoticed. Jelisa made her way back into the kitchen and continued to put the groceries away. "So, I need to tell you something, but you have to promise you won't get mad."

Shamar knew what she was about to say. He let out a sigh.

"What you blowing for? You don't even know what I'm getting ready to say."

In a low tone, Shamar said, "Yes, I do. Go ahead and say it."

"See, I knew I shouldn't have said anything. Forget about it."

"Naw, go ahead, Jelisa. Stop playing with me," he said sternly.

She knew he was going to snap when she told him that she had loaned her mother more money. She didn't want to have to explain it to him when he found out on his own because that would have made things worse. "All right, so, you know I've been staying with Mama, right? Well, I had to loan her some money to help with the bills. She promised—"

He cut her off before she could finish. "Really, Jelisa? What did I tell you about that? Stop letting people use you like that. I mean, hell, you've only been there for a couple weeks, and it's already starting. You know good and well that if she needs to borrow the money, she has no way of paying it back."

Shamar tried not to go too hard on her, but he wanted to make his point very clear. He was fed up with Jelisa's family using her and making her feel obligated to help them just because she was staying with them.

"But . . . Yeah, I know, baby, but she is letting me stay with her. What am I supposed to do?" Jelisa pleaded, trying desperately to calm him down as she could hear him getting more and more frustrated.

"Get your own place like I told you to!" he snapped. He could hear himself getting loud, and people in the call center he was in started giving him looks. The makeshift room was simply a large tent that had been furnished with cubicles and fifteen phones for soldiers to use. There was really no privacy, and that made it even more important that Shamar compose himself. He had no idea who could have been listening in.

"Look, I'm not trying to be mean about it; but if you want them to stop taking advantage of you, you're going to have to stand up for yourself. They are going to have to respect the fact that it's not just your money they are getting; it's ours, and you have to make sure I'm cool with it first."

When she heard that, Jelisa raised an eyebrow, surprised at the tone he had just taken. *Who does he think he's talking to?* "What do you mean, I have to make sure you're cool with it? You ain't my daddy, and I'm not about to be running to you every single time I need to buy something just to get permission."

Shamar couldn't believe what he'd just heard. Was she really coming at him like that? Not wanting the conversation to end on a bad note, he chose not to respond with the same attitude she was giving him. He took the phone away from his ear and held it to his chest. Then he looked up at the ceiling and gathered himself. Finally, he responded with, "Jelisa, don't play me like that. Have I ever told you that you had to have my permission to do anything?"

She got quiet. The silence over the phone was deafening; you could hear a pin drop. Jelisa cleared her throat but didn't respond. She knew her attitude was uncalled for and she had no comeback.

Feeling vindicated, Shamar followed up with, "I didn't think so. Baby, I told you anything you need is yours to have. It's just money. God! I'm really not trying to have us arguing every time we talk. I need you to hold me down while I'm gone, so we have to have an understanding. All I ask is that you be smart with the money and don't be out there trying to ball out, you feel me?"

Hearing Shamar assert himself gave her chills. As hard as he could sometimes be, he was a pushover when it came to her and Mya.

She hated feeling like she had to take charge in situations so being put in check reaffirmed her confidence in him. "All right, Shamar," she whispered in submission.

Shamar grinned and added, "And please go get your own spot and get out of her house. That way she can't ever say you owe her nothing."

After all of the going back and forth, it dawned on Shamar that he hadn't even asked about his daughter. He missed his little princess like crazy. "What's up with Mya? How is she doing?"

Jelisa looked over at her tiny body that had fallen asleep on the living room couch, and she said, "She's good. She misses you. She's in the living room knocked out on the couch. You want me to wake her up?" She turned to walk into the living room.

"No, I'll talk to her next time. I got to get off of here anyway and get ready for this little thing we've got. But I'm going to try to give you a call in a couple days. It might be hard to catch up with you because of the time difference, but I'm going to try. I love you."

Neither wanted to hang up, and Jelisa's eyes started to well up as she considered the thought of never hearing from him again. "All right, babe, I'll let you go. I need to finish putting this stuff away. You make sure you call me and don't try to be no hero. I'll be waiting for your call, okay? Talk to you later. Love you."

"All right."

Shamar hesitated to hang up and slowly they got off their phones.

That Friday morning, Shamar got called to accompany a tank unit as their medic on a mission. Often times in the past, while they were back in the States, different units would request Shamar to come and teach classes to their medics. He was only a sergeant, but it had only taken two years for the unit to start talking about promoting him again. As a soldier, he was on the fast track to senior leadership, and his reputation from other missions with his last unit preceded him.

As the team lined up their vehicles to head out, Shamar silently prayed. He never went out on a mission without doing so. Some called him superstitious; others thought it was because of where they were deployed that shook him. Either way, it gave him comfort knowing that he had sent a prayer up, and that was enough.

The mission was to escort the unit commander out into the city to meet with the local government. While on the convoy heading to the meeting location, Shamar was floored by the amount of poverty he witnessed. So much so that he thought, *man, folks in the States have no idea what being poor is. These people literally don't have a pot to piss in and they making it work.* It was a sobering experience to see the kids play in the streets, women walking together going to the market, and the men sitting back in front of the small clay houses, talking politics.

The air was humid, and the sun beat down on their Kevlar-covered vehicles. Shamar could hear over the radio that they were approaching the mayor's office. Immediately, reality set in and, as the four HMMVs came to a halt, everyone's attention turned to the two-story buildings that surrounded them. Locals peeked out of windows and stood on balconies with displeased faces. They investigated the Americans walking in front of their homes dressed in full battle gear carrying M-16s in the ready position. Two of the convoy vehicles positioned themselves at the nearby corners, and Shamar and two other soldiers stood guard in front of the doors.

A young boy started approaching them. Shamar was the first to notice him. He nodded his head at the other soldiers, drawing their attention to the unexpected visitor. The young Iraqi boy was about 200 yards away, and he was carrying something tucked under his left arm.

Shamar turned in the boy's direction, and in a commanding voice he shouted, "Hey, stop right there!"

The boy didn't break stride as he walked another fifty yards. Whether it was on the streets of Michigan City, in his home, or Iraq, Shamar hated having to repeat himself. With all of the rumors that the rebel insurgents were recruiting kids to get close to soldiers and blow themselves up, killing the soldiers as well, he wasn't taking any chances. Shamar shouted even louder this time "*Qiff!*" which meant "stop" or "halt" in Arabic. The boy continued to walk another fifty yards or so before the other soldiers began to yell, echoing Shamar.

Finally, when he was just over a hundred yards away, the boy stopped. He placed the item that was tucked under his arm on the ground in front of him and took a step back. All of the soldiers were tense, their weapons now aimed at the thin frame of this child who couldn't have been any older than twelve or thirteen.

The sun was hitting Shamar on the side of his face, his adrenaline started pumping, and there were beads of sweat streaming down his forehead and temples. Time seemed to stand still at that moment as he contemplated the possibility of the item being a bomb. Jelisa's and

Mya's faces flashed in his mind as he considered the thought of not being able to see them again. Just as the moment came to a climax, with everybody waiting on Shamar's next move, the boy took a step forward and kicked the item. As it came closer and closer to their position, the soldiers took cover behind their vehicles.

Shamar, with brief hesitation, took a closer look as it approached; and then he looked back at the other guys with a grin on his face. "Y'all, it's all good, man. Little dude just wants to play with us; it's a soccer ball." They all responded in disbelief with laughs and sighs of relief as they walked back over to where Shamar was standing. Shamar stopped the ball with his foot and gently kicked it back to the boy, who was now fifty feet away walking toward them.

The boy picked the ball up and walked up to Shamar and said in broken English, "Chocolate?" They all laughed as they were used to the kids asking for candy, especially chocolate.

Shamar went back to his vehicle to retrieve some of the chocolate candy pieces that he normally took with him to persuade the kids to trust them. He said under his breath, "Thank you, Lord." The other soldiers began talking to the boy and kicking the ball back and forth with him while Shamar walked back to where they were standing. This had been an intense, yet funny, situation for them all and it reminded him how important his family was to him.

Ten minutes passed, while they were entertaining the young boy, before the commander and his assistant emerged from the building. "Mount up!" he shouted, eager to hurry and get back to camp.

Shamar and the others gave the young boy high fives. The boy stopped him as he turned away. He reached into his pocket and pulled out a green string of yarn with brown beads on it. His face lit up with the biggest smile Shamar had ever seen on a kid. He stretched out his hand to Shamar with the handmade necklace dangling from his tiny fingers. The look in his eyes would be something the soldier would never forget. He took the gift from the boy, nodded his head, and bid him farewell while getting back into his vehicle. Shamar was surprised at the boy's gesture. But the more he thought about it, he knew it could have just been a ploy by the boy to get his guard down.

The team then proceeded back to the camp to debrief from the mission.

***

Back in the States, Jelisa was embarking on her own special mission to find an apartment for her and Mya. She found a spot not far from her old neighborhood, off of Coolspring Avenue. It was a nice two-bedroom apartment, just big enough for them. Unfortunately, the celebration of her new move was short-lived as she dealt with the backlash from her mother and sisters.

Sandra wasn't totally sold on Jelisa and Shamar getting married in the first place, let alone her moving away with him. Even if he was her husband, Sandra didn't trust any of her girls in the care of any man. One could only imagine how anxious she was, knowing that Jelisa would be away from her with her grandkids without her supervision. She did not think she was ready to be on her own. Jelisa never informed Sandra that she was going to sign the lease for the apartment, so she never saw it coming.

Jelisa got up early Saturday morning and went down to the leasing office at the complex she was moving into. When she returned to Sandra's, she walked through the front door with the keys and paperwork still in her hand. She was met by Sandra as soon as she shut the door. The amount of arguing and yelling that followed would put you in mind of an intense spades game being played by a bunch of high-strung, heavily inebriated middle-aged men.

"So when were you going to tell me that you were moving, Jelisa? Was I just supposed to come home one day and find all of your stuff gone or what?" Sandra laid into Jelisa, making sure she experienced every bit of displeasure she was feeling.

"Mama, you got a lot of nerve getting mad at me for wanting to move out," Jelisa responded while stuffing the keys and papers in her coat pocket and then throwing it on the living room couch next to her. She further defended herself, saying, "Mama, you moved out of Granny's house when you were seventeen. I'll be twenty in December. I have my own family to worry about and I'm not going to let you, or anybody else, come before that."

Sandra took a couple steps back and sized Jelisa up, still in disbelief that her child had spoken to her that way. But she knew something Jelisa didn't think she knew and it was finally time for her to throw it back in her face. "Please, child, don't you dare stand there and act like you're all innocent when you know good and well you weren't thinking about that when you lied to Shamar about Mya being his."

Jelisa's mouth dropped, and her eyes got big. She couldn't believe it. This was an all-time low, even for Sandra. But Jelisa wasn't about to be bullied any longer. It had been going on for too long. This wasn't the kind of treatment she'd expect from the woman who gave birth to her. Not willing to let Sandra have the last laugh, Jelisa stood her ground and proclaimed, "You know what, Mama? I would have thought, out of all people, you would be the one I could trust. But for you to throw something like that in my face, especially while I'm dealing with Shamar being gone, is just messed up. I'm glad I'm getting up out of here." Jelisa stormed toward Sandra, heading down the hallway to her room. She looked right past her mother as she got closer.

Sandra stood with her head down, knee-deep in a pity party with only herself in attendance. Jelisa bumped shoulders with her, not wanting to redirect her route to avoid her. The tension in the house was thick.

As Jelisa began packing her things and Mya's, she began to cry. Mya had been the one thing that held the relationship between her and Shamar together. She dropped to her knees next to the bed and sobbed as her mind took her back to the previous year when the rumor had begun to spread around the city that Shamar wasn't Mya's father. It was a terrible experience for her, not only because she was afraid Shamar would find out or believe the rumors, but because she would have to explain what had really happened. She had a secret that no one knew about and she was willing to take it to her grave.

Sandra, who was still standing in the hallway, now overcome with guilt, listened in anguish to her daughter cry her eyes out. She turned and headed back to Jelisa's room and stood in the doorway. She walked over and bent down, grabbing Jelisa by the hand and helping her to her feet. As they stood toe to toe, the sound of small footsteps echoed down the hallway. They both looked attentively toward the door as Mya emerged, rubbing her eyes and grasping her favorite Winnie-the-Pooh blanket. Mya walked in and headed straight to Jelisa with her arms reaching out, begging to be picked up. Jelisa tried to smile and stop the tears from falling, but they wouldn't stop.

Sandra motioned for Jelisa to sit down on the bed. They both sat. Jelisa sat Mya down on the floor as she turned toward Sandra, wiping her face. "Mama, why do you hate me so much?"

Sandra's heart sank as she considered the thought that Jelisa may actually be right; maybe she did hate her.

"Daddy was the one who left, not me; and it wasn't my fault, either. So why out of the four of us do you take him leaving out on me? You've always treated me different. I just don't understand, Mama," she pleaded with Sandra, still crying, and hoping for an explanation.

Sandra looked at Jelisa and hesitated before answering. "Well, honey, I don't think that there's anything that can be said nor done that will change things. Whatever happened between me and Pete had nothing to do with you. I treat you the way I do because I see so much of myself in you and I don't want you to repeat the mistakes I made. I know I haven't been the easiest to get along with lately, but I've made a lot of sacrifices for you girls. I just don't think you appreciate it."

Just when Jelisa thought she was finally getting some closure, Sandra flipped the script on her and went back into her manipulative state. "See, you think you're better than me because you're married now, and you're moving away. I gave up everything for you and you walk around my house with your nose turned up like I'm some bum on the street."

The tears coming from Jelisa's eyes suddenly dried up, and her sadness turned to rage. It took everything in her not to haul off and swing on Sandra.

Jelisa stood up, looking her mother in the face. She turned around and resumed packing, now furiously. She didn't want to waste another minute being in her mother's presence. The woman standing next to her was a complete stranger, and Jelisa wasn't comfortable around people she didn't know.

Sandra stood by helplessly as Jelisa continued to gather her things. After five minutes, she finally gave up and left the room, going back into the living room. She plopped down on the couch in front of the TV, trying to act like she didn't care and attempting to elicit a reaction from Jelisa as she walked out.

Once Jelisa was done packing the two suitcases she had, she was determined to get out of Dodge as soon as possible. She left everything else behind as Shamar had given her the freedom to get whatever she wanted for her new place. Without even looking in Sandra's direction, Jelisa stormed through the living room and out the front door with Mya on her hip. As she juggled the two suitcases and Mya, struggling to get to her car, her sisters looked on from the upstairs window. Meanwhile, Sandra stood in the living room smoking a cigarette, peeking through the curtains. The whole house was in suspense as they watched Jelisa drive away.

While she was on her way to the new place, the Ashley Furniture delivery guy called and said he was down the street from the complex. This was a welcomed phone call. She needed something to cheer her up, and having an apartment full of brand new furniture would definitely do the trick.

Hours later, after the delivery company had unloaded and assembled her new furniture, Jelisa and Mya were set and glad to finally have their own place. After a fun-filled evening of Chinese food and Princess Tiana, Jelisa and Mya were getting ready for bed when her cell phone rang. She hoped it was Shamar calling to check on them before they went to bed. Mya's eyes lit up as she heard her mother's favorite Mary J. Blige ringtone. Mya ran over to the coffee table and grabbed Jelisa's phone and, with the most determined look on her face, she ran back to her mother with her phone in her hand, reaching out to give it to her.

"Hello?"

"Hey, what's going on?" a voice said on the other end of the phone.

Jelisa tried to catch the voice, but she couldn't quite figure out who it was. There was a lot of noise in the background, music playing, and people talking. It sounded like there was a party going on.

"Who is this?" Jelisa inquired with her eyebrows frowned up, wishing the secret caller would reveal himself. She removed the phone from her ear and looked to see if she recognized the number, but it said Private. She must have been distracted by the fact that Mya had the phone because she normally didn't answer calls from blocked numbers. "Look, whoever this is, I'm not in the mood to be playing on this phone. Who is this?"

The deep baritone voice on the other end chuckled as if he found it amusing that she was starting to catch an attitude. Toying with her further, he said, "So you mean to tell me you don't recognize my voice? Has it been that long?"

Jelisa had no clue who she was talking to. There was no telling who he was and how he got her number.

Having had enough, Jelisa hung up and turned her phone off. She wasn't going to entertain anybody calling and trying to be funny all night. She and Mya finished up for the night and, after a nice, warm bath, she changed into her PJs, which consisted of Shamar's basic training

PT shirt and a pair of boy shorts. After putting Mya to sleep, Jelisa turned her phone back on to check her messages just in case Shamar did, in fact, try to call while she was ignoring her unwanted caller.

Chapter Five

The next morning was a busy one for Jelisa. Not only was Saturday a busy day for the shop, but she was also without a babysitter due to what went down with Sandra. By the time they got to the shop, it was jumping. Donny had a line of people in the waiting room, and Jelisa had a full day's worth of clients scheduled. An orchestra of hair clippers and blow dryers filled the shop and set the mood for the day. Jelisa, on the other hand, was not looking forward to the day that awaited her. Missing Shamar and having to be in the shop all day with Mya was the worst combination.

As she took Mya over to the waiting area, Donny greeted her and watched her as she walked past, eyeballing her short, petite frame. "Hey, baby girl, what's up? How you liking the new place?"

Jelisa walked over to her chair, which was now right next to Donny's, and set her bag down underneath the counter. She had originally been located on the other side of the shop with the stylists, but she felt more comfortable being in the midst of all the guys. Females who usually frequented the shop were just too messy. In most cases, she felt at least the guys were honest about what they wanted. "I'm good," she said as she turned and set up her workstation. "I love the new place, just trying to get used to being on my own and not having a babysitter."

Donny really had no interest in her new apartment. He was really trying to test the waters to see if she was in the right state of mind for him to make his move. He stared at her slim waist and thick thighs as she turned toward the mirror and adjusted her smock string around her waist. The devilish look in his eyes suggested that he had nothing but bad intentions. "So what you getting into this weekend? I'm thinking about having a little kickback at my crib. You want to come?" he asked. He grinned, hoping that she would say yes. He figured with her husband being gone, all he had to do was get her to let her guard down, and from there it was only a matter of time until he had her right where he wanted her.

"See, there you go, Donny. You know I'm married. I don't even get down like that. You ain't about to have me over your house drunk and looking stupid." She looked at him, halfway smiling but dead serious. Shamar might be in Iraq, but he still had enough friends in the city. So many that it wouldn't take long for him to find out about anything she did.

Donny, not easily discouraged, looked back at her with all determination and said, "Naw, baby girl, you know it ain't even like that. Everybody from the hood is going to be there, so you'll be safe."

She wasn't buying it. She waved him off and called for her first customer to come take a seat. Being surrounded by men at the shop all the time gave her a different perspective when it came to them. However, Donny was a different type, one unlike any she had ever dealt with on this level. Jelisa had only been at the shop for a little over eight months before she left the first time and the only thing she had concluded concerning Donny was that he was a man whore.

"Yeah, I don't know about that. We'll see," she said, blowing him off. Jelisa was not very trusting of men, especially in Michigan City. Everybody knew each other and their business, and it never took more than a day for rumors to spread like wildfire if they were started by the right person. That was exactly how things had gotten blown out of proportion when rumor had it that Shamar wasn't Mya's father.

Jelisa was working at a salon in Eastport, a section of town on the east side, not far from the interstate. While she was in the back room getting ready to start her day, she overheard two females talking about Shamar. Not wanting to let on that she heard what was being said, she stayed in the cut and continued to listen to see what all they had to say about her man.

"Girl, he is fine, though; and I heard that he got that D. I don't know why he still messing with Jelisa," one lady said to the other. It was common for females to display just how thirsty they were.

The other responded in agreement, "Yeah, girl, I know. I heard that too. I wish he would come my way. It would be a wrap. But, girl, I heard he just married her 'cause he didn't want her messing with anybody else. You know these dudes out here are hella dirty. They don't have no problems messing with their homeboy's baby mama." They both turned their lips up and nodded their heads in agreement with each other.

"You right, girl, 'cause I heard that ain't even his baby. My cousin told me she used to mess with this dude from Gary and he supposed to be her baby's daddy. See, that's what I be talking about; these ratchets be out doing they dudes *hella bad, and then they get mad when they come running to me."* The first lady declared this with such sincerity that you would have thought that she actually believed the nonsense that was coming out of her mouth.

Jelisa fought the urge to say anything because she wanted to see what else they had to say. She hated when people gossiped, especially when it involved her.

The second lady, feeling justified in her remarks, echoed her feelings. *"I'm telling you, girl, she don't know what to do with a man like him. Now he done went into the military, so she got his butt stuck taking care of her and that nappy-headed little girl. I don't get it."*

That last statement struck a nerve with Jelisa. The craziest part of the whole situation was that she didn't even know these women. The hatred they shared for her seemed genuine as they carelessly discussed her personal life. Jelisa grabbed the closest thing she could find, which happened to be a handheld blow dryer sitting on a storage shelf. She grasped it by the handle and came from behind the wall with her hand cocked back. She walked over to the left side of the chair that the second lady was sitting in and, without breaking stride, Jelisa cracked the first lady across the face.

"Trick, do you even know me?" she shouted.

The lady fell forward out of her seat onto the floor and, right before her friend could stand up to assist her, Jelisa swung back and clocked her in her mouth with the blow dryer as well. They wrestled and punched and kicked each other until some of the guy customers stepped in and broke them up. The two ladies cussed Jelisa up and down, threatening to call someone to come handle her. They weren't expecting this little five foot four inch woman to be able to throw hands like she did. She handled both of them like she was a dude.

Fixing her hair and her clothes, Jelisa, with the now broken blow dryer still in her hand, composed herself and checked both of them, saying, "You sluts better keep my name out of your mouths before I slice both of y'all ugly faces up. You don't know me or my man and don't you ever let me hear you had anything to say about my child. Try me if you want to!"

Jelisa stood her ground that day, but that was typically how she handled situations like that. Growing up with all sisters and being the smallest, she had to learn real quick how to defend herself. Her "pop off" mentality was another reason Shamar was attracted to her. The fight in the salon cost Jelisa her chair, and she was forced to find somewhere else to set up. After a couple trial runs at other shops, she ended up at Platinum Designs.

Donny knew that eventually Jelisa would start feeling the effects of being alone and he was determined to be there to comfort her. He left it alone for the time being; he didn't want to completely turn her off. As the day came and went, it was business as usual at the shop. As she was packing up her things and getting Mya ready, her phone rang. With one hand slightly grasping Mya's little fingers and the other with two bags dangling from it, Jelisa managed to get to her phone. She saw it was another out-of-town number. Thankfully, it wasn't a private number her mystery man might have called from.

"Hello?" she said with the phone pinned between her ear and her shoulder. She opened the car door, dropped her bags on the floor behind the passenger's seat, and waited for Mya to navigate her way into her car seat.

"Hey, baby girl, what's up?" It was Shamar on the other end. It was a much-needed phone call as the day had taken a toll on her.

"Hey, baby. I'm so glad you called. I was hoping to hear from you yesterday."

"Yeah, we had a couple missions going on and I couldn't get away. How you doing? Did you get settled into your new place yet? I wish I could have been there to help." Shamar's concern was comforting. His being there would have made all the difference.

"I know. Me too. I'm all moved in, but things with Mama got crazy yesterday."

Shamar shook his head and started massaging his temple as he prepared for the details of the dramatic event that went down. "What happened?" he inquired.

"So, you know Mama's been acting real extra lately? Well, she went off when I told her I had already found us a place to stay and I didn't need her help with it. She started trying to make me feel guilty about leaving and made it seem like I owed her so much I should be willing to stay and help her out. It pissed me the hell off." Jelisa was glad to have somebody to vent to even though she knew there was nothing he could do about it.

"Really? Man, that's crazy. How she gon' get mad at you for wanting to have your own space? I mean, usually most parents can't wait for their kids to grow up and move up out of their house. That's just crazy." Shamar knew that Sandra would try something sneaky while he was gone, but he didn't expect her to go to the extent of making her own daughter feel bad about trying to be a wife. "Well, honey, don't let that stuff get to you. You know your mother and how she can be, so just keep doing what you're doing. I appreciate you taking care of things while I'm gone. How was your day at the shop?"

Jelisa held the phone between her shoulder and ear as she buckled Mya into her car seat and got in the driver's seat. "It was all right, I guess. You know I had Mya with me the whole day since I can't take her to Mama's anymore. She didn't act up too much," she said.

She turned the car on and proceeded home, continuing the conversation. "I'm just tired. I need a break from everything. Can we go somewhere when you get back? I mean, like a vacation, somewhere we haven't gone before."

"Yeah, of course, honey, just let me know where you want to go, get the information together, and we'll make it happen. What are your plans for the rest of the week? Do you have a lot of appointments?"

Jelisa was liking this conversation with Shamar. He wasn't usually this inquisitive. He was showing so much concern for her and Mya that she thought maybe being away from them was doing him some good. He was showing so much interest in the things she was dealing with. "Well, I've got a few appointments lined up. I'm pretty set for the week. Donny is supposed to be having something at his place for everybody at his spot. I told him I wasn't sure if I was coming. But, other than that, I'm not doing much."

Shamar didn't like the sound of that at all. He knew Donny and his reputation. He wasn't really cool with her working at his shop, but he figured she wasn't dumb enough to let him catch her slipping. "Jelisa, listen to me when I say this: I'm not trying to tell you what to do, but you need to watch yourself around that dude. Don't let him fool you and have you doing something you'll regret."

She didn't like him trying to warn her about anybody, especially considering all of the so-called female friends he had. "Shamar, please, with all of those females you say you just cool with. I ain't stupid; he ain't got nothing I want or need. I'm not thinking about him. I just want to get out and do something."

"I understand, but don't say I didn't warn you. It's not you I don't trust; I know you got me. But I also know that deployments can take a toll on couples and I don't put nothing past anybody. It's him I don't trust because he don't have to have any loyalty to me. You feel me?" Shamar took issue with people who preyed on lonely women. Even though he trusted Jelisa, he had to take into consideration that she'd held him down this long and she wasn't like all of the wives of soldiers he knew. Most of the people he knew who were married were already finding out their wives were messing around. That in itself was responsible for Shamar's concerns.

While he was getting ready to make his next point, a voice came across his handheld radio saying they needed him back at the medical tent immediately. He didn't want to alarm Jelisa, so he played it cool as he attempted to get off of the phone with her. "All right, Jelisa. I love you, and tell baby girl I said I love her. I gotta go. I don't mean to rush off of here, but I have to tend to something real quick."

"Okay. I love you," Jelisa said with disappointment in her voice.

"Love you too, babe."

The phone went dead, and all she heard was the dial tone. She didn't know what that meant. Was he just trying to get off the phone with her? Did something bad just happen? Her wheels starting turning, and she became anxious as she considered that he was at war so it could've been anything. She didn't like the issue of him not being able to talk for long periods of time. Talking here and there was starting to bug her and, as much as she knew he cared about what she was dealing with at home, she understood he still had a job to do. As much as she wanted to, she couldn't be mad at him for doing his job.

As Jelisa pulled into parking lot of the apartment complex, she threw the phone on the passenger's seat. Irritated that their conversation was cut short, she now had an attitude, and she wondered if it was going to be this way the whole time he was gone. She unloaded Mya and her bags and made it into her apartment. She turned on cartoons for Mya to keep her busy while she went and got dinner started.

Chapter Six

Block

It was just after 10:00 a.m. Fourth of July weekend: the perfect time for Block to come home. Michigan City was humming with the news that he was about to hit the streets. As he walked down the sidewalk leading away from the prison, there was no welcoming party. There was no parade, and it didn't seem that anybody cared that he was even out.

Block made his way down Willard Avenue wearing the same white tee and black Dickies he wore when he was booked in. He was carrying a brown paper bag containing all of books and pictures he'd collected over the years. As he made it close to his old hangout spot, Pullman Park, memories of hooping flashed in his mind. Block walked to a nearby bench and sat down on the edge of the backrest. Everything seemed foreign to him. The Westside Liquor Store was gone. The corner store had been burned down. This wasn't home to him anymore.

Suddenly, he could hear the bass thumping in the air. He didn't see any cars around but, as loud as it was, he figured it had to be close. Whipping around the corner was a black BMW with windows tinted as dark as night. The blacked-out twenty-twos wrapped in Pirellis caught his attention. The car parked and sat momentarily before the driver's side window slowly rolled down, releasing a cloud of cigar smoke.

Block, now growing anxious, climbed down from the bench, adjusting his pants in case he had to make a quick exit. As the window rolled down, it slowly revealed a face he hadn't seen since the first day of his trial. Bloodshot eyes seemed to disappear in the backdrop of a face as dark as night. His grin displayed yellow teeth tinted with years of tobacco smoking and coffee drinking. This barefaced, pudgy goon was the only thing that stood in the way of Block enjoying his newfound freedom. When he realized who it was, his blood began to boil, and anger seized his mind.

Sitting in the car was a dirty narcotics detective named Alonzo Garrett. Detective Garrett was a certified creep who wouldn't hesitate to pin charges on anybody he saw fit just to stroke his pride. He got a hard-on from hemming people up.

"So, I heard they let an animal out of its cage today. I just had to see it for myself. What are you doing over here on my side of town, you dirt bag?" Detective Garrett said, taunting Block, knowing he had a reputation for being a hothead.

Here he go with this mess. Man, ain't nobody got time to be bothered with this airhead, Block thought. "Bruh, is you serious right now? I ain't two hours out the joint and you already on my head? Man, kick rocks. I ain't got no rap for you. I'm on my way to see my people," he snapped back.

During his trial, Detective Garrett was instrumental in him almost getting hit with the murder charge. He hated what Block represented. The Foster family was one of the most well-connected families in the state. Not for drugs or guns, but real estate. In the late eighties Block's grandfather, Roland Foster, won a $15 million lawsuit against a steel mill. He was forced to retire early after an accident caused by the company's negligence. Grandpa Foster settled in court and began buying up premium real estate around the region, some of which was now coveted by the local government.

To Detective Garrett, people like Block didn't deserve to be so well off, and with a couple million set aside for him, he was now Garrett's number one enemy.

"Why don't you go find a trap to raid or somebody to plant some dope on? 'Cause me and you don't have nothing to talk about. As a matter of fact, am I being detained?" Block asked, giving him a cold stare. With all of his time on lockdown, he knew one thing he made sure to do was get familiar with the law.

"No, punk, you're not being detained, but don't push your luck. I've been itching to yoke somebody up," Detective Garrett countered, knowing their visit had run its course.

"Really, fam, you've been itching? TMI. You can keep that to yourself. But, if there's nothing else, I'm gonna be on my way. I have a schedule to keep, as I'm sure you do too," Block taunted.

Without waiting for a response, Block turned and walked off, cutting across the field toward the main road. Unmoved, Detective Garrett laughed it off, rolled up his window, and sped off. "We'll see each other again real soon," he said under his breath. The crooked detective had his mind set on finding the weak link in the Foster family, and he assumed it was Block. Only time would tell.

***

After meeting with his parole officer, Block managed to find a pay phone, which he used to call his sister. He didn't mind walking the twenty-plus minutes from the prison to the courthouse, but he wasn't about to head to the east side by foot.

As he waited for Latoya to arrive, he couldn't help but feel a bit slighted by the fact that no one came to get him. That was the least he expected, since everyone knew he was coming home today. Fifteen minutes passed, and Block was beginning to think she had forgotten about him. Latoya told him to look out for a gray Lexus sedan and, just as he pictured it in his mind, she pulled into the parking lot. As he walked down the sidewalk, all he could think about was the amount of time that had passed by without him being able to touch his sister.

Just as he made it to the second step, a beautiful young woman rushing to get to an appointment nearly knocked him down. She was dressed in a dark blue and gray pinstriped business suit. The skirt that stopped just above her knees hugged her curves perfectly. Her honey blond weave blew in the wind as she breezed past him. A pair of Chanel frames consumed her face they were so big. Slightly distracted by her voluptuous shape as she walked away, Block was left speechless and didn't have a chance to respond verbally. He just continued down the stairs as his attention was quickly diverted back to Toya as she stepped out of her car.

A flood of emotion overcame the two of them, and Block dropped his bags to embrace his big sister. Picking her tiny five foot two inch frame off the ground, he hugged her and spun her around, grateful for all she had done over these last fifteen years.

"Boy, look at you! You got big since the last time I saw you. What you been doing?" Toya said as they separated. She stood back with one hand on her hip, shielding her eyes from the sun with the other.

Proud that his big sister noticed how he'd bulked up, Block grinned and struck a jailhouse pose. "Well, you know what it is. You took care of me. If it weren't for you holding me down on my books, I don't know what I would've done. I definitely wasn't eating the garbage they called food. But what up with you? I see you all tatted up and weave all down your back. That's how you living?" Block said jokingly.

Toya was never the flashy-label whore type most females in the city were. After she was able to join in the family business, she figured it was necessary to look the part. Toya still knew how to sniff out a bargain, even when it came to her newfound love for stilettos and Remy hair. Toya responded with a smile, "Well, you know your big sis is always the star of the show. We in business, baby brother, so let's get you right. I'm sorry I wasn't there to pick you up. I wasn't expecting them to let you out so early. I know you felt some type of way about that, didn't you?"

"You know I did, Toya. Had me feeling like I was going to be out here popped with nowhere to go. But I appreciate you coming through for me all this time," he said, picking up his bag of belongings.

They drove toward the east side to Toya's condo on the edge of town. She made it a point to take the side streets, giving Block a chance to see how much the city had changed. "This is crazy, Toya. Where is everything? They done tore down Crown Liquor for real?" Block observed in disappointment. It was a totally different place; a bright morning on the Fourth of July weekend and nobody was out. It was so depressing.

Toya answered candidly, saying, "Yeah, bro, it's crazy out here. The police raiding all the hangout spots, and this new mayor seems to have a point to prove. Everybody they lock up is getting numbers hung on them. I'm telling you, the struggle is real and folks don't have a clue what to do. Luckily for us business is booming, and these industrial properties are going cheap. So how soon are you ready to get to work? We already got your office space set up."

Block drummed his fingers on the center console, still contemplating what was considered to be the "New Michigan City." He glanced over at Toya as she blew through several stop signs before pulling over at Walker Park. This was the location right down the street from where his homeboy Boomer was shot when they were younger. Toya knew this was probably the first place Block would want to visit. "You think you know me, huh?" he joked. "Thanks, sis. I really appreciate it. You coming?"

"Naw. Take your time. I'm going to run around the corner to my girl's house. You good for a few minutes?"

"Yeah, I'm straight," he said, exiting the car.

"All right. I'll be right back."

Block couldn't help but get emotional when he saw the RIP BOOMER tag he did still faintly visible on the basketball court. As he traveled back in his mind on an excursion down memory lane, he heard a faint voice coming from the other side of the park fence. Lo and behold, a sight for sore eyes stood in the middle of the street. The gorgeous young lady's face looked very familiar but Block couldn't put his finger on it. He had no idea where he knew her from.

She stood about five foot two with brown skin tanned to perfection. Her smile, bright enough to put the sun to shame, invited him to come closer to investigate. As she stood with her hands on her hips, her shoulder-length hair blew in the wind. Block couldn't help but feel like he was starring in a movie the way seeing her made everything around them come to a standstill. *Shawty thick as hell. Where do I know her from?*

He walked over and stood at the entrance of the gate, leaning on one arm against it. "Shawty, where do I know you from? You look so familiar. There's no way I can forget a smile like that," Block inquired, slightly flirting.

"Seriously, Block, you don't remember me? Has it really been that long? Wow, I guess that kiss really didn't mean anything, huh?" the young lady teased, trying to refresh his memory.

As Block thought harder, her words and voice began to match up and he realized who he was talking to. It was his old friend Bria, a twenty-five-year-old go-getter. When she mentioned a kiss, his attention was drawn to her thick, heavily glossed lips that turned him on the more she licked them.

"Bria, is that you? Word. Shawty, you're a whole woman now I see," Block said in an attempt to compliment her. He quickly realized just how long it had been since he had seen Boomer's little sister, Bria Cash. However, she wasn't the innocent little preteen who used to follow them around back in the day. She was all woman, and Block couldn't take his eyes off of her. This was awkward for him, as he was conflicted about how to feel about her. On one hand, she was his best friend's little sister and, although he had long ago left this life, he still had respect for him. On the other hand, she was obviously a grown woman; and fifteen years was a long time without being this close to a woman.

Bria walked closer, meeting Block at the entrance. She paused and smiled, giving him that side eye before speaking. "So, I'm kind of hurt that you didn't remember me, Block. What's up with that? When did you get out?" she asked, playing with the small gold cross pendant hanging from a thin gold necklace around her neck.

"Naw, it's not even like that, Bria. I just didn't recognize you, that's all. It's been a long time," he said as he came around the gate, joining her on the opposite side. "I just came home this morning, and you know the first thing I had to do was come show my respects to my bro. Give me a hug, though. It is good to see you after all these years. What you was, like, ten years old last time I saw you? How have you been?" Block inquired, still amazed at how gracefully she'd developed.

He wrapped his arms around her shoulders, and she rested her head on his chest. Immediately tears flowed from her eyes. As they separated, he noticed the sadness on her face. "Bria, what's wrong?" he inquired with a look of concern.

"I'm sorry, Block. It's just that being here in this place and with you, it just makes me think about my brother and how much I miss him," Bria answered.

In most people's eyes, Block and her brother Boomer had always been best friends. There was rarely a moment you would see one without the other. To Block, that was the only reason Boomer was no longer with the living.

Bria composed herself and continued answering his question, saying, "Yeah, it has been awhile. I just turned twenty-five last month, so you owe me a birthday present, too," she teased, bending down to tie her shoe.

Block tried to compose himself and keep from giving into the temptation to check her out. That was a nearly impossible task but, out of respect for Boomer, he resisted. When she stood up, Block, nodding his head, motioned for Bria to walk with him. As they walked and continued to catch up, the two shared fond memories of Boomer and the time when he kissed her on the cheek. To him it meant nothing. She was just a kid, and he was just being nice in response to her giving him a Valentine's Day card. Unbeknownst to Block, Bria carried that kiss in her heart from that day forward. She was heartbroken when she sat in the courtroom listening to him being sentenced. In her eyes, what he did for his sister solidified her love for him. The whole time he was away she dreamed of the day she'd see him again. However, Block would never know, seeing as he didn't receive one letter or picture the whole time. Bria loved him from a distance.

Block's life was now beginning to piece itself back together as he accepted his newfound freedom. Finding love was the last thing he was looking for, but it had been waiting for him for fifteen years. Neither Bria nor Block knew how long it would take for him to discover this gift.

***

Later on, back at his new spot after a long shower attempting to wash the filthy feeling of prison off of himself, Block draped himself in one of the many custom suits Toya had hand-picked for him. It fit perfectly and, as much as he wasn't thrilled about it being his day-to-day wardrobe, he was impressed by how good he looked.

The grumbling of his stomach disrupted his brief fashion show, and he stood in a large walk-in closet surrounded by full-length mirrors. He had heard about a new spot on the boulevard called Kevin's and, after years of gut-wrenching prison food, Block longed for some down-home cooking.

On the kitchen counter lay a car key with a note underneath it written by Toya that read:

Hope you like it . . .

As he opened the door on the far end of the kitchen that led to the garage, Block didn't know what to expect; but if the suits she had chosen for him were any indication, this new whip would be fly. In the middle of the garage sat an all-white Yukon Denali. The size alone of the SUV stunned Block, and he couldn't wait to hit the streets in it knowing that it would officially mark his reintroduction to the city.

Driving back through the east side was a trip, to say the least. Everything had changed so much so that most of his high school friends now had teenage kids of their own. Not only did he feel out of place, Block felt old. As he pulled into the parking lot of Kevin's Blockhouse, he instantly felt unsettled. Anxiety shot through his body; something didn't feel right. Just then he peered into his rearview mirror and, lo and behold, that same black BMW sat off in the corner of the parking lot. "Come on, man, seriously?" Block said audibly.

As he parked and exited his truck, Detective Garrett followed suit. Adjusting his jacket and tie, Block turned and leaned against the vehicle with his arms crossed. "Say, bruh, don't you have something better to do with your time than to be keeping tabs on me? I mean, seriously, I'm starting to think you have some kind of infatuation with me or something," Block said condescendingly.

Detective Garrett frowned, obviously irritated, and answered arrogantly, "Listen, convict, don't think that because you can throw on a suit and charm your PO I'm not watching you. You are still scum, and I'll be watching your every step. See, what you don't understand is no matter how much money you throw around town, this city belongs to me. You Fosters don't run anything; you never have and never will!"

Block was still confused as to why this dirty agent was so fixated on him and his family. He pushed himself away from the vehicle and squared up with the detective, saying, "Look, man, I don't know what the hell you're talking about. I ain't been on these streets in fifteen years. There is nothing you can say that I've done to you to have me in your crosshairs. So I'm really gonna need you to fall back, man, 'cause you're really starting to piss me off." Block wanted so bad to knock the arrogant smirk right off Detective Garrett's face.

However, he didn't back down, but he responded sharply, saying, "Go ahead, Foster. I'm getting a hard-on just thinking about throwing you back in a cage for another fifteen years. Just give me one reason."

Now fed up and growing more irritated by the second, Block decided this little visit of theirs had gone on long enough. "Look, man, either cuff me or kick rocks. We're done here. Pardon my back," Block proclaimed as he turned and walked away, not giving him another thought.

Detective Garrett scoffed and turned, walking away, lighting a cigar. "Yeah, okay. I got you, convict," he said under his breath.

Feeling disgusted by the interaction with Detective Garrett, Block rushed home to change clothes and cars in an attempt to get a fresh start. He was feeling more like the Chevy at this point, and he just wanted to be around some positivity.

Chapter Seven

After getting off of the phone with Jelisa, Shamar rushed over to the unit's medical tent to help tend to some kids who had been hurt by a roadside bomb. The sight of kids in their condition messed him up. He tried not to throw up when he saw a young girl with half of her left leg blown off. There was blood everywhere, and she was beginning to go into shock. Shamar was usually calm during these instances, which was why they called him to assist.

There was also a boy who looked to be about twelve or thirteen with shrapnel covering most of his body. His face was covered in blood and dirt as he clung to life, struggling for his next breath. When Shamar approached the boy to tend to his wounds, he noticed there was something familiar about him. As the minutes passed, the boy grew weaker. Shamar tried talking to him to reassure him it would be okay. He had never been this shook about something like this.

He had seen dead bodies and people wounded before but never to this extent.

Shamar tended to him further, getting assistance from another medic. He turned to call for a syringe of morphine to help ease the pain. With the severity of the wounds he had, it was unlikely the young boy would make it. Shamar administered the morphine, and it quickly kicked in. As the boy struggled to hold on and Shamar scrambled to stop the bleeding coming from his chest, he grabbed on to Shamar's sleeve. The boy wouldn't let go and with everything in him he begged God to save the boy. The boy gasped and took one last breath. Within those few seconds, his and Shamar's eyes met and immediately it hit him where he recognized the boy from. He was the boy he had played kickball with in front of the government building just days before.

The boy's eyes drifted down just beneath Shamar's chin as he saw the necklace he had given him dangling. He looked back up at Shamar, closed his eyes, and stopped breathing.

Shamar's heart broke; he stood up feeling defeated and walked over to the side of one of the vehicles. He had tried everything he knew to do, and nothing could save him. Tears streamed from his eyes as the past ten minutes replayed

over and over again in his mind. He questioned
to himself, "Why would God let something like
this happen? He was just an innocent kid."

The girl the other medics had been working
on had already passed away; there was nothing else anyone could do. Shamar walked off,
heading back over to their living quarters to
clean himself up; but it was like everything
around him stopped moving.

It was a sobering experience for him, and
word quickly got around camp about what had
happened. Omar didn't waste any time coming
to see about his friend. When he arrived at
Shamar's bunk, he was still shaken up. He had
his Bible open on his bed with a picture of Jelisa
and Mya next to it. As he sat there in a daze,
he had a blank stare in his eyes. It took Omar
calling Shamar's name a couple of times before
he responded.

"Shamar. Hey, bro, you all right, man? I heard
what happened. It must have been crazy."

Shamar looked at Omar and nodded his head,
but he didn't speak.

"Look, man, you know we see this kind of stuff
all the time, bro. You can't beat yourself up like
this."

Shamar glanced at him out of the corner of his
eye and, in a low voice, he said, "He was just a

kid, man. How do we justify something like that? I mean, like, that could have been my kid or one of my cousins or something. I can't even wrap my mind around it. I just don't get it."

"I know it's hard, man, but you gotta remember we're at war and things like this happen. I know that sounds harsh, but you know as well as I do that they use those kids against us. For all we know, he could've been setting the bomb up to take one of us out, and it went wrong. I mean, dawg, you just don't know. But you can't let this stuff eat away at you. You need to call Jelisa. You gotta talk to somebody and get your mind off of it, feel me?" Omar pleaded with his friend, hoping to calm him down.

Shamar heard everything Omar was saying, but it did nothing to change how he felt. He appreciated him being there for him, though; he could always count on Omar to hold him down.

Shamar sat for several hours replaying the earlier events in his mind repeatedly. Before he knew it, night had come, and he still hadn't left his bunk. He eventually took Omar's advice and went to the call center the next day to try to get in touch with Jelisa; but when he called, she didn't answer. He figured, with the time difference, she must have been busy. It was almost noon in Iraq, so it was still early back in the States.

Shamar didn't realize how much time had gone by. It seemed like he had just talked to Jelisa not long before. He never got around to calling her back that afternoon. The whole thing took such a toll on him that, after a few hours, he decided he didn't want to talk about it. At the end of the day, he was still a soldier and casualties, whether young or old, came with the territory.

At the end of the work day, Shamar went over to the chapel to sit and think. He was exhausted and, after all of the crying and stressing out, that was all he had the strength left to do. He found solace in being able to let off some steam and ponder everything that was important to him.

After twenty minutes in the chapel, Shamar caught back up with Omar. They went to the chow hall for dinner before going back to their quarters to bed down for the night. Shamar spent that night writing a letter to Mya, explaining the world to her. Shamar wanted to be the best father he could be, which to him meant preparing Mya for the potential heartbreak she might have to endure later in life. If there was one thing the Army taught it was that life is too short to go through ignorant of its pitfalls. In his heart, he hoped to be able to shield her from as much as possible, but he had another ten months before he could get back to her.

For the time being, he would just dream about all of the things they were going to do together as a family. The trips to SeaWorld and Disneyland, teaching Mya how to ride a bike, and even going horseback riding like Jelisa always wanted. Although he wasn't big on these kinds of things, he knew it would mean a lot to them, and he promised, so that was enough. Shamar continued thinking about these things until he finally fell asleep.

Chapter Eight

The week went by fast for Jelisa and, when Friday morning came, Donny was already in his bag, acting just as cocky as ever as he made his way to the shop. He had every intention to get her to his spot and get a couple of drinks in her. When she arrived at the shop that morning, she wasn't in a good mood. The stress of not being able to talk to Shamar when she wanted to, along with not talking to her mother, was getting to her. The loneliness was starting to set in, and she craved some adult conversation that didn't consist of gossip and negativity.

It was just before 9:00 a.m., and Donny was pulling up as Jelisa was getting out of her car. He parked, got out, and made his way toward her. "Hey, baby girl. How you doing this morning?" he asked with a big grin.

She wondered why he was so chipper this early in the morning. "Hey, Donny, I'm good. How you doing?" She forced the conversation as she wasn't feeling like dealing with his flirting.

Although, after being rushed off the phone with Shamar and then not hearing from him for the rest of the week, it didn't seem like such a bad idea. She walked around to the passenger's side of her car and helped Mya out of her seat and onto the sidewalk.

"Oh, I'm good, ma, getting ready for this kick-back tonight. You coming through?" he asked, holding the door for her as she and Mya walked up the stairs.

"I don't know yet. You know I don't get down with most of these females you have working in here. These sluts are too messy for me and you know I got a low tolerance for BS," Jelisa said, looking back over her shoulder as she made it over to her workstation. She set her bags down and picked Mya up, placing her in her styling chair as she began touching up her recently done cornrows.

"I feel that," Donny said, nodding his head as he took out his clippers and began oiling them to prepare for the day. "Don't let that stop you, though. I mean, you're in here most of the week, and now you've got li'l mama with you. I know you need some time to yourself. Just think about it. I'm not going to bug you about it anymore. I think it's about time you got out and did something." Donny was working his magic. He had a way with his words of convincing females that his intentions were pure and he was harmless.

Jelisa was starting to overcome her attitude after she took a few sips from her Starbucks green tea. Sometimes that was all it took to put her in a better mood. Like most people are with coffee, you never wanted to mess with her before she had had her morning tea.

As the morning progressed, Jelisa started feeling guilty about not speaking to her mother all week. Mya had been waking up the last couple of mornings walking around the apartment and calling for her granny. She resented her mother for what she said and even more for the fact that she hadn't attempted to contact her. Jelisa knew that if she didn't reach out, Sandra never would. She was just that stubborn, and it wasn't fair to Mya to not be able to see her granny or aunts because of what they were dealing with.

During her lunch break, Jelisa called her mother to see if she could break the ice. As the phone rang, her stomach was in knots. Not knowing how she would respond, she braced herself for a rude response.

"Hey, Jelisa," Sandra said nonchalantly as if nothing had ever happened. She didn't let on, but she held grudges. One could never tell if she was still dwelling on something because she could mask it so well.

"Hey, Mama, how you doing? Your grand-daughter has been walking around my apartment calling your name," Jelisa teased, trying to be funny about it.

"Oh, yeah? Well, tell her Granny misses her too. I would like to see her, if that's okay with you," Sandra said, appealing to Jelisa's sensitivity to the nature of the situation.

It was working as Jelisa put away the hesitation that was keeping her from further engaging in the conversation. She was keeping Sandra at arm's reach just in case she still had an attitude with her. "Yeah, Mama, you can see her. As a matter of fact, why don't I just let her stay over for the weekend?" Donny's words were quietly whispering in the back of her mind as she thought about the peace and quiet she could have with no kid in the apartment for a couple of days. It was still up in the air whether she would go to his get-together that night.

"Okay, that's not a problem. I wanted to take her to the circus tomorrow anyway, so that works out perfectly. What time are you getting off today? We need to talk."

Jelisa wasn't expecting that. Although she knew it was inevitable, Sandra didn't usually make the first move when it came to apologizing. Perhaps she finally realized how serious their issues really were. In her mind, Jelisa didn't think that was the case. "I should be out of here by five. I only have four heads today so I should be done around that time. I'll stop by after I get off. Okay?"

"All right. I'll see y'all then. Call me when you're on your way."

"All right, Mama. Bye."

One thirty came around, and Jelisa had just finished up her second client of the day when her cell phone rang. She answered, as usual hoping it was Shamar. "Hello?"

"Hey, Jelisa, what's up? You busy?" Shamar said with a bit of excitement in his voice.

"Yeah, baby, of course. What's up? Why do you sound so happy?"

"I got presented with an award today for my work on our last mission. Plus, I found out I'm getting promoted to E-6 this week. My commander told my supervisor he thought it was time. It's conditional because I still have to go to leadership school when I get back. But they gave me the option to take my stripes now and start making that E-6 pay; or I can wait until after school, and they will give me back pay. I'm amped, babe!" Shamar was grinning from ear to ear, proud that he had done something worth bragging about.

"Oh, wow, baby! That's great! I'm so proud of you! I'm glad to hear things are going good for you over there. I was waiting for you to call me back after we got off last time, but I'm okay now since I know you've been working hard. You know we—" Jelisa's other line beeped and, thinking it might be her mother, she didn't bother to look at the caller ID. She told Shamar to hold on while she answered the other line.

"Hello?"

"Hey, sweetheart, how you doing?"

Jelisa's heart dropped. It was that same raspy voice that called her before. "Look, whoever this is, you need to stop calling my phone. I don't play them type of games. Stop calling me!" she shouted; then she hung up and clicked back over to her other line. "Hello, Shamar?"

"Yeah. Who was that, your mom?"

"No. Some dude keeps calling my phone talking like I'm supposed to know him. I asked who he was and he acted like I'm supposed to recognize his voice. Shamar, you know I don't like people playing on my phone." Jelisa was noticeably disturbed by the call from this anonymous person. It was starting to scare her.

"Well, honey, I don't know; maybe you need to get your number changed or something. I mean, how do you think he got your number?"

"Shamar, I don't know. I don't even give my number out, especially not to some dude I don't even know. Anybody who has my number is usually a client, and they are all females. So I don't know, but it's really starting to irritate me." Jelisa's hand started shaking and, as she sat in the back room of the shop, she heard the door beep. It was her two o'clock appointment. She didn't want to end the conversation since it had been a few days and there was no telling when she'd hear from him next. She motioned for her client to go ahead and seat herself.

"Baby, what's going on with you? I know I haven't called in a few days. The last time we talked I tried to explain it to you, but honestly, that whole situation I just went through had me in another place. Seeing somebody die is never an easy thing, especially when they're so young." Shamar could feel himself getting emotional, and before tears could fall he caught himself and changed the subject. "I miss you so much, you know that?"

Jelisa's face lit up, and a huge smile covered her face. She needed to hear that. It wasn't that she doubted him, but she was beginning to feel overwhelmed with the thought of something happening to him. The fact of the matter was they both needed the reassurance. As much as she didn't want to let him go Jelisa knew she couldn't leave her client waiting too much longer. She reluctantly spoke up and whispered, "Well, baby, I need to let you go; my client just got here. I love you and congratulations on your award and stuff."

"All right then, thanks. You just make sure to be safe leaving tonight. Watch your back; you know there are some crazies walking around out there. I love you, and I'll try to call you tomorrow. Good-bye."

"Love you too. Good-bye, baby."

Shamar was feeling good about his award and upcoming promotion. It meant a lot to him that his unit recognized his efforts, and it didn't hurt that there was some extra money involved. While heading to the chow hall for a late snack, he met up with Omar, who congratulated him, shaking his hand and patting him on the back.

"Congrats, homie! I heard the good news. How does it feel?" He chuckled, proud of his partner in crime.

"Man, it's a cool feeling. It definitely took my mind off li'l dude; you know what I'm saying?"

"Yeah, I feel you. You talk to wifey lately? How she doing?"

"She all right, man, I guess. She told me some dude keeps calling her phone, got her bugging out. You know I don't like that stuff," Shamar said, shaking his head.

As they walked into the dining area, they got in line for the sandwich bar. It stayed open twenty-four hours a day for the different soldiers who had late-night and early morning missions. They continued their conversation as they made it through the line.

"Yeah, man, I know how you are about that stuff. But you ain't on the streets anymore so let that go. I know you'd mess around and call home and try to put a hit out on somebody over her and baby girl," Omar commented, making light of the situation. As he spotted a table to sit at, they made their way to the middle of the dining area.

They heard a faint voice saying, "Shamar. Shamar." They both turned around to investigate. A tall, dark-skinned female corporal with big, gorgeous brown eyes and cute dimples made her way across the room toward them.

"You know her, man?" Omar asked Shamar.

Shamar squinted his eyes, trying to make out her name tag as she got closer. "Naw, man. She looks familiar, but I don't recognize that last name." Her name tag read GREENWOOD.

That name didn't ring a bell, but Shamar felt like he knew her from somewhere. The Army was a small world; you were likely to run into somebody you knew in the strangest places.

The young lady got within a few feet of them and said, "Jackson, you don't remember me? It's Tamika Johnson. Well, Greenwood now. How you been?"

Shamar scrambled to think back to where he knew her from. "Johnson. Tamika Johnson. Oh, snap!" he said as it dawned on him. He remembered now; he went to high school with her. "Tamika from Michigan City? Dang, girl, I haven't seen you in years. What you doing over here? I didn't know you joined the service." Shamar's eyes got big as his mind took him back to the eleventh grade, when he first met her. She was a grade behind him, but he had a crazy crush on her back then.

"Yeah, it's me. Been a long time, huh? Look at you. Still got them pretty brown eyes, huh? Yeah, I joined the Marines right after high school. I'm a medic and my unit just got here from California for this joint taskforce. What you been up to?"

Once they all sat down at the table, Shamar realized he was being rude and hadn't introduced her to Omar. "My bad, Mika; this is my guy Omar. Omar, this is my girl Tamika from back home."

They shook hands and smiled as she turned her attention back to Shamar. "So, what you been up to? I heard you got married. What's up with that? I didn't think you were the marrying type," she said jokingly with a smile on her face.

Shamar wondered what the odds were of him running into her this far away from home. "Yeah, I know, right? But I did it; been married almost seven months now. What about you, Greenwood? What's up with that?" Shamar pointed at her name tag with a smirk on his face.

"Yeah, that's a long story right there. I won't be married much longer. My knucklehead husband acted a fool on me during my last deployment and messed around and got some chick pregnant. You know I couldn't let that slide."

Both Shamar's and Omar's faces had stunned looks on them. Unfortunately, that was commonplace among married couples in the military, especially with the Army and Marines. "Wow, that's crazy, ma," Omar said in disbelief. "Homie did you dirty like that? He had a whole baby on you? Man, that's foul."

Shamar shared his shock and disbelief. He looked at her and, for a second, he flashed back to high school when he was going after her. The look on Tamika's face was numb; it seemed like it didn't even bother her. Shamar lost himself in her eyes and wondered why somebody would treat a person, who was so beautiful, so ugly.

The breaking of a drinking glass in the background snapped him out of his daze. He continued with the conversation, stating, "That is dirty, Mika. How you holding up, though? I know that's got to be hard, especially being over here."

Tamika shrugged it off, not wanting to show that it was actually still bothering her. "I'm good, y'all; it's nothing I can't handle. Men and women make their own decisions, and you just have to take it for what it is. I'm just glad I found out before I gave that fool any kids. You talking about crazy, it would have been a totally different story if I had ended up being somebody's baby mama. Anyways, on to a new subject. What's going on with you, Shamar? What have you been up to these days?"

Shamar and Omar both laughed at her tactless attempt to change the subject and get the attention off of herself. "I'm good, man. Like I said, I'm married, and I got a four-year-old little girl. But we straight. Ain't too much changed. I just had to get away from MC. I felt like I was stuck in like a black hole. People were either hustling or making babies; and, of course, I was doing both. So, either way it went, I was not going to come out on top. The Army saved my life, real talk."

Shamar was proud of his testimony; and as much as he and Jelisa went back and forth, he knew she was a rider.

Tamika had a smirk on her face, displaying her doubt. This wasn't the Shamar she knew. Married life must have really made him soft.

"Why you looking at me like that?" Shamar said, puzzled at the awkward look.

"You know why," she answered while clearing her throat, trying to dull the grin on her face.

"Girl, stop playing with me. What you mean I know? How am I supposed to know?" Shamar joked.

Tamika moved her chair over, closer to him, so that her thigh was touching his thigh. She was close enough that he could smell her perfume; the fragrance drove him crazy. He played it off and looked her in her eyes as she leaned over and frankly said, "You went soft."

Omar clowned Shamar; he busted out laughing, stomping his foot and clapping his hands. "Wow. Bruh, she got you on that one," he teased.

Not the least bit shaken, Shamar laughed it off. "Naw, sweetheart, never that. I just got tired of dealing with the same tired females. Everybody screwing the same people; my homeboys had kids by the same chicks. I had to find me one chick I knew wouldn't cross me, and that's what I got."

Tamika couldn't believe it. This ex-player and ex-hustler had been reformed. "Well, good for you. I'm happy for you," she said. Although she didn't believe a word he was saying, she didn't want to push it any further. She still had feelings for him, but he was taken. While most women seemed to be drawn to men in his position, she wasn't one of them. The Marines had made her heart tough; and, after being cheated on by her husband, she was callous toward men. Shamar was cool and all, but the most he could do for her was give her a good nut. That would only be if he was single, because she refused to cause another woman the same pain she had experienced.

"Well, I appreciate it, Mika. Everybody has to grow up at some point. I'm hoping I get to go home on R and R next month to surprise her. Know what I mean?"

"Yeah, I know what you mean, but be careful with that."

"What do you mean be careful? Careful about what?" Shamar didn't know what she was getting at, and he had a confused look on his face.

Omar chimed in, saying, "Bruh, you know what she's talking about. Be careful."

Suddenly, it dawned on him what she actually meant. "Oh, man, my bad; I don't know where my head is at. Yeah, I know what you mean. I'm good, though."

Tamika didn't really think he got what she was alluding to. "Shamar, you pop up on that girl unannounced if you want to and you might walk in on something you don't want to see. I'm just saying."

Omar concurred, nodding his head. "Yeah, bruh, that's real talk, especially coming from a female. I know you got a good girl and everything, and she'll ride for you, but we all know what these deployments can bring out of a lonely woman. We've seen it."

Shamar was starting to get uncomfortable. He hated when people tried to get in his head, especially when it came to Jelisa.

They could see the irritation on his face, so Tamika tried to reel the conversation back in. "Look, I'm just trying to keep you from the same stuff I went through. I'm not trying to say that your girl is doing something; I'm just telling you not to set yourself up, that's all. Anyway, it's getting late. I need to get out of here," she said, standing to her feet.

"Okay. What you got going on tomorrow?" Shamar questioned.

"Nothing. I'm not going to be here long. I'm on my way back to the States. I'm just here to help set up things before the rest of the unit comes."

"Man, how you pull that one off?" Shamar was amazed that she was able to weasel herself out of a deployment. That was not an easy thing to do.

"Well, let's just say I know all of the right people. I made sure that it would work out for me so that I didn't have to be deployed the same time as my husband. But when you get back to the States, look me up." She grabbed a napkin and wrote down her phone number and e-mail address.

Shamar and Omar both stood up, and he gave her a quick hug. Omar shook her hand, and they wished her a good night.

"I got you. I'll get with you when I get back. Good seeing you again," Shamar said as Tamika walked away, waving good-bye to them.

As she walked off, both Shamar and Omar checked her out and looked at each other. There was something about the way that combat uniform hugged her curves. "Boy, I tell you what, Omar; I swear if I weren't married, shorty could get it," Shamar said.

"Yeah, man, I know that's right. She thick as hell, bro. How you miss out on that?" They both laughed about it and resumed eating their food.

It was refreshing to see somebody from home so far away, and Shamar wished that he had had more time to catch up with her. At the same time, he was thinking about Jelisa, wondering what she was doing. The warnings Omar and Tamika gave him still haunted him, as much as he tried ignoring them.

They finished up their late-night snacks and went back to their own quarters to get some rest for the next morning. The past week had its share of ups and downs but, all in all, it turned out to be a decent week for Shamar. He only hoped that the next month would have the same results.

Back at home, Jelisa was finishing up her last client when Donny made one last attempt at convincing her to come by his place that night. Jelisa had thought about it, and she concluded that she needed to get out of the house. She wasn't about to be one of the Army wives who didn't have any friends and didn't do anything but stay in the house and work. But before she committed to hitting the town and having some fun, she had to get past the hurdle that was her mother. She would have to endure the snide remarks and weird looks as they mended what remained of their relationship.

After she had finished with her client, she cleaned up her station and got Mya together to get ready to go. She'd finished early, and it was close to four thirty. Mya had fallen asleep on the couch in the back, so she was half asleep as they proceeded to walk out the door. Jelisa looked back to tell Donny good-bye. Not wanting to miss his chance, he stopped what he was doing and walked over to her.

"Hey, Jelisa, hold up for a second." He got extra close to her, to the point where she had to take a step back to put some space in between them.

She frowned her face up and leaned away from him. "Dang, boy, you awfully close, aren't you? I'm getting ready to leave. What's up?"

Donny, still grinning, backed up and responded, "Hold up, baby girl. You coming through tonight or what? The party won't be the same without you." He chuckled.

"Look, I don't know yet. Maybe. I still have to find a babysitter. I'll try, okay?"

Partially satisfied, Donny nodded and accepted her offer. He handed her his address, which he had already written on the back of one of his business cards in anticipation of her saying yes. She looked surprised and cracked a smile, slightly impressed by his confidence and persistence.

"All right, I'm gone." She and Mya headed to the car and loaded up to head over to Sandra's.

As she got close to the house, her stomach started doing flips. She was filled with anxiety, hoping that this wouldn't be another blowup. In an attempt to level the playing field, Jelisa sent her older sister Shawnie a text, asking her to be downstairs when she got there, just to mediate. Shawnie was the second oldest and the one who would most likely be able to keep everyone calm. Having her there gave Jelisa a sense of security, knowing Shawnie wouldn't let things get out of hand.

It was just before five o'clock when Jelisa arrived in front of the house. As she opened up the door and unbuckled Mya from her car seat, Mya had excitement all over her face. After she helped Mya out of the car and onto the sidewalk, Sandra appeared from behind the front door. Jelisa watched as Mya's little feet carried her up the sidewalk and into her grandmother's arms.

"Hey, Granny's baby, come here," Sandra said with a big smile on her face. Jelisa stood back for a minute, letting them enjoy the moment. Sandra bent down to pick Mya up; while doing so, she glanced over at Jelisa but didn't say anything.

Jelisa started thinking back on the reason it was so hard for her to understand why her mother didn't seem to like her. She hadn't told anyone about it, and it killed her that she had carried this secret around for years. As she stood there in a daze, daydreaming about the past, she felt a breeze pass by the back of her neck. It gave her chills and shook her out of her stare.

"Y'all come on in," Sandra said, waving at Jelisa.

When they got inside the house, Shawnie was sitting on the couch and Jelisa's baby sister, TT, was sitting at the kitchen table, playing on her cell phone. Shawnie looked over at the entrance to the kitchen and called out to TT, "Hey, T, take Mya upstairs for me, would you?"

TT turned her phone off, got up, and grabbed Mya's hand, leading her upstairs.

Jelisa walked over and sat down next to Shawnie. "What's up, girl? Thanks for coming down," she said, patting Shawnie on the thigh.

"Girl, it's okay. I know how Mama can be," Shawnie whispered under her breath. "Mama, can you come sit down so we can talk?" Shawnie said to Sandra, who was now standing in the kitchen by the refrigerator, staring out of the window over the sink. She let out a deep sigh as she could tell they were about to drop something heavy on her. As she made her way into the living room, she paused frequently as she attempted to light one of her Newports.

"All right, what's up? What do y'all need to talk to me about?" Sandra sat down on the love seat directly across from them, flicking the ashes from her cigarette into the ashtray on the coffee table. Sandra couldn't stand when people tried to corner her and get her in her feelings. She hoped that they wouldn't get too deep on her and start bringing up old stuff that no one could do anything about anyhow.

Jelisa cleared her throat and sat up, leaning toward her, and said, "Mama, I just need to know why you hate me so much."

Sandra's posture changed as she leaned forward, placing her forearms just above her knees. She took a deep breath and then a pull from her cigarette and mumbled, "Um hmm."

"See, Shawnie, I knew she was going to do this. She ain't trying to hear nothing I have to say," Jelisa said, looking over at Shawnie.

"Just go ahead and say what you need to say, Jelisa. Don't worry about all of that. She's here, isn't she?"

"Mama, I just don't see what I did that was so wrong that you have to treat me the way you do. I mean, you don't act this way toward anybody else, but as soon as I come around or I question something, you say then it's a problem." Jelisa could feel herself getting worked up. The heel of her right foot started tapping rapidly on the floor, and her knee bounced up and down rhythmically.

"Look, Jelisa, I'll admit I have resented you because of your dad. When he left, it was the hardest thing I had ever experienced before. Your father always favored you over me, and I will admit that burned me to my core." Sandra's face grew grim as she relived the past verbal and emotional abuse handed down by Pete over the years.

Jelisa was amazed at the amount of anger and disgust that was written all over Sandra's face. "Mama, I get that, but I was a kid. How can you blame me for stuff Daddy did? That was between you and him; I didn't have nothing to do with that."

"Jelisa, I don't expect you to understand. He always treated you better than your sisters. And I hated the way he took your side whenever you and I got into it. Ugh!" Sandra grunted. In retrospect, Jelisa kind of knew the real reason Pete treated her and TT different than Shawnie and her oldest sister, Monica. Shawnie and Monica both had different fathers and Pete was Jelisa and TT's biological father. Pete never felt like he could say much to the two oldest girls because he wasn't their father.

"Mama, see that's what I'm talking about; you act like I did something to you. What did I do?"

"What did you do?" Sandra shouted and stood up, leaning toward Jelisa and pointing her finger in her face. "It's because of you that I could never keep a man in this house, anyway. You did the same thing with Reggie."

Jelisa heard that name and became furious. Reggie was Sandra's former live-in boyfriend. He moved in a couple of years after she and Pete divorced. In the girls' eyes, Reggie was a nasty old man. He was a retired steel worker with a bad drinking problem and an unnatural attraction to young girls. Sandra was so heartbroken by the breakup with Pete that she just wanted a man in the house.

Jelisa jumped up and leaned over the table, pointing her finger right back at Sandra. She shouted with everything in her, "Mama, how dare you bring up that pervert! You know—"

Right then, Shawnie pushed the coffee table out of the way and jumped in between them, holding Jelisa back. "Jelisa, stop; don't do it. Y'all just sit down and cool out."

Sandra dropped her hand and stepped back. With a calm voice, she said, "I'm calm, I'm calm, but ain't no child of mine going to talk to me like that in my house."

Shawnie interrupted her, "Mama, she didn't even say anything."

"I know what she was about to say. And she is not about to keep throwing that in my face." Sandra was referring to Jelisa saying multiple times that she didn't feel comfortable around Reggie.

"Mama, please stop playing with me right now. You have no idea." Jelisa started pacing back and forth in front of the front door. Shawnie could see the situation was about to go from bad to worse real quick.

"Stop playing with you? Little girl, who do you think you talking to? I will—"

Jelisa interrupted her, getting right in Sandra's face. "You'll what, Mama? I'm sick of you. I can't take this no more. I hate you!" she shouted with great conviction. "Mama, you don't know how hard it is for me to look you in the face and not scream. All of this time you've been blaming me for Daddy leaving you and treating us different. He actually loved us, and that's what was different. You never loved me or TT; you always hated us. And now you have the audacity to stand here and blame me for Reggie leaving, too. I swear to God, you got hella screws loose."

Shawnie moved quickly to push Jelisa back toward the front door. Her five foot frame jumping around and trying to get past her was an indicator that there was nothing Shawnie could do to calm her down at this point.

Sandra stood square toward Jelisa, still smoking her cigarette, which was now down to the butt. "What you trying to say, Jelisa? Huh? Go on and get it off your chest." Sandra was slowly slipping into her manipulative state, trying to guilt Jelisa into letting it go.

The anger boiled inside Jelisa, and suddenly the floodgates of her eyes burst open as she screamed in torment, "He raped me, Mama! Okay? He raped me!" Jelisa dropped to her knees, cupping her face in her hands.

As she sobbed desperately, Shawnie looked over at Sandra with disgust and anger. "You knew this, didn't you?" she said.

"What? Shawnie, stop that." Sandra barely showed any reaction to Jelisa's claim as she tried convincing her that she had no idea it had happened.

Shawnie wasn't buying it. She helped Jelisa up from the floor, walked her to the kitchen table, and sat her down. "Jelisa, baby, I'm sorry," Shawnie said as she rubbed circles on Jelisa's back. Shawnie turned her attention back to Sandra, walking over to within a foot of her. She stood face to face with her. Calling her bluff, she said, "Mama, I know you; and you're not about to stand here and play stupid. Look me in my face and tell me you didn't know."

Sandra looked away, barely making eye contact with her. "I'm not about to do this with y'all," she proclaimed.

"Oh, yes, the hell you are. Mama, I love you; but I promise to God, it's gonna be me and you up in here if you keep lying. You know what? Don't even answer that 'cause I know you did. I know you, and you trifling for that. What kind of mother are you?" Shawnie wanted so badly to slap the piss out of Sandra. Instead, she called TT downstairs, gathered Mya and Jelisa, and they all left and went back to Jelisa's apartment.

As they drove off, Sandra went and poured herself a glass of vodka and sat at the kitchen table. She was ashamed that she had let something like that happen to one of her girls. Her pride wouldn't let her go after them, and she figured Jelisa wouldn't answer if she called anyway. She sat at the table for the rest of the night, smoking and drinking until there was nothing left in the bottle.

Chapter Nine

When the sisters arrived at Jelisa's apartment, the whole mood was somber. Jelisa hadn't said anything the whole ride home; she just cried and stared out the window as Shawnie drove her car for her. TT followed them in her own car. Jelisa was in rare form this evening; no one had ever seen her as angry as she was. It wasn't out of the ordinary for her to pop off, but this had Shawnie and TT worried about what she might do next.

The sisters gathered around Jelisa in the living room on the couch, each trying desperately to get her to talk. Mya stood next to her mother, clueless as to what was wrong, but attempting to make it all better by bringing her dolls and placing them in her lap.

"Jelisa, you have to talk about it, honey. I know this is hard. We had no idea," Shawnie said, taking Jelisa's hand into hers.

"Yeah, Jelisa, tell us what happened," TT chimed in.

Jelisa remained silent for a moment, and then slowly lifted her head to whisper, "I don't want to talk about it, y'all. I'm sorry I didn't say anything, but I didn't think anybody would believe me."

Shawnie and TT sat by helplessly as Jelisa contemplated on whether to fill them in on the details. She hesitated for a moment, and after taking a long, deep breath, she proceeded to explain. "All right, y'all, so long story short, Reggie waited one night for everybody to go to sleep and then he came into my room. He covered my mouth so I couldn't scream and he threatened to kill everybody. I didn't know what to do." Her tears increased as she relived the horrible moments of that night. "I called Shamar and told him to come over to stay with me 'cause I was terrified to leave my room."

Shawnie's eyebrows rose as she remembered the events that followed that night. The morning after that tragic event took place, Sandra walked into Jelisa's room to find her and Shamar fast asleep. The sight of her fifteen-year-old daughter in bed with her boyfriend sent her into a rage. She flipped out on both of them, banning Shamar from ever coming over her house again. She grew to resent him as she began to see Jelisa draw closer to him and further away from her.

Shawnie was in the next room listening as her mother scolded the two. She tried to warn Jelisa that she might get caught but after everything that had happened she didn't want to press the issue. In Shawnie's opinion, her mother would never be okay with them being in love with any man. She envied her daughters and the way their father cared for them. Shawnie would do anything to protect her sisters but when it came to men there was only one way she knew to deal with them and prison orange would never look good on her.

"Jelisa, I'm so sorry. I wish there were something we could have done. Does Shamar know about it?" Shawnie asked, trying not to push her too much.

Jelisa shook her head and replied, "There's no way I could ever tell him. What man would ever want me after something like that? I'm damaged." She looked over at TT, knowing that she could relate. She knew firsthand what Sandra's hatred for them looked and felt like. Their mother had no shame in showing her jealousy toward her girls. TT, being the youngest, not only got more attention from their father, but her sisters now became her protectors. "Look, y'all, do me a favor and stay here tonight. I need to get out of this apartment, and I don't want Mama anywhere near Mya. She's on thin ice with me. I don't even want to see her right now."

Jelisa knew she probably wasn't stable enough to go out, but her usual response to feeling low would be to curl up next to Shamar. Being stuck in the house was a constant reminder that even with her sisters and Mya there with her she was still alone. She had no desire to be around the people from the shop but, at this point, it was far better than sitting at home, staring at the TV. Jelisa still wasn't totally sure about going out but staying home just wasn't an option.

Her request didn't quite sit right with Shawnie. She knew her sister and going out in such a vulnerable state would only lead to her putting herself in a situation she would regret, especially when it came to men. Jelisa was strong-willed, and Shawnie knew that there was no way to talk her out of it. "All right, Jelisa, but are you sure? Is your head in the right place to be trying to go out right now?" Shawnie asked.

"Look, Shawnie, I'm good. I just need to get out. I'm not going far, and I won't be out long. I'll probably just go to this little thing Donny is having for everybody who works at the shop. It's at his house, but I promise I'm okay. I just need something to get my mind off of this craziness. Y'all know how I get. I'm not going to be able to stay in this house all night."

Against their better judgment, the sisters agreed to stay behind with Mya while Jelisa went out to clear her mind. "All right, Jelisa," Shawnie said. "I know we can't change your mind about this, but don't think we're not going to deal with this eventually. You can't avoid it, honey, or it's going to continue to eat away at you. Forget about Mama. You need to get some closure for yourself."

Jelisa was growing impatient, and her face told exactly how she was feeling inside. She felt nasty and worthless. No one had ever made her feel so low. Staying in the house meant she would either have to sit and relive those feelings or possibly be subject to her sisters drilling her with questions. She had gone years without having to deal with it so one more night wouldn't hurt.

Jelisa left the living room and went into the back to her room to change clothes. As she stood in the front of her dresser, staring at herself in the mirror, her face covered with dried tears, she wished that Shamar was there with her. With him around, it was the only time she felt safe. But she knew that eventually she would have to tell him the truth. Michigan City was too small of a city for things like this not to get around. For now, she was content with handling things on her own.

***

Having decided to get out and free her mind of the pain she had just relived, Jelisa decided to make an appearance at Donny's party. She was in her own world as she got into her car and made her way out to South Gate, where he lived. Whenever he threw a kickback, everybody came out. People went out and bought new 'fits and hit the carwash to make sure they came through flossing. As Jelisa made her way onto the street Donny lived on, coming from the windows of his house was the sound of hard-hitting bass and the laughter of slightly drunk men and women.

When she parked her car and proceeded to walk toward the house, the aroma of blunts and joints filled the air. People lined the sidewalk and the driveway. As she made her way up the stairs, she was greeted by the who's who of the city. She was well known, and every head turned her way when she stepped in the place. Jelisa didn't keep too many females close to her, so she was usually alone. Unless she was accompanied by her sisters, she didn't usually have an entourage.

She navigated her way through the sea of people, exchanging smiles with all of the ballers and ignoring all of the thirsty women and their rolling eyes. The smoke was thick in the living room as she made her way to the back deck where she could hear Donny's voice cracking up in laughter. She looked around for a friendly face but saw none. Determined to enjoy herself, she decided to stay. At the corner of the deck, Donny stood in an all-white tailored Steve Harvey suit with baby blue snakeskin ankle boots and a hat to match. Donny seemed to have cleaned up pretty good.

"I didn't know he had it in him." Jelisa laughed to herself. Donny stood across from her, looking as good as ever. Jelisa suddenly felt something drip down the inside of her thigh and noticed her arms were covered in goose bumps. What was happening? This feeling that had come over her was different from any she had had being around Donny before.

She tried shaking off the fact that just the sight of Donny tucked over in the corner made her moist. Against her better judgment, she took a couple more steps in his direction. She paused when he removed the shades from his face.

He licked his lips, rubbed his perfectly shaped-up goatee, and nodded at Jelisa. "So you decided to grace us with your presence, huh, baby girl? You looking hella sexy in that dress." Donny admired her skin-tight red dress and stiletto heels, which seemed to make her legs look like they went on for forever up her dress.

His attempts to seduce her with his words were working. She found herself captivated by his whole persona, and all the time she spent trying to be faithful to Shamar seemed to not even matter anymore. Her inhibitions began to subside as she imagined what it would be like to spend the night with him. The next thing she knew, she was face to face with Donny, taking in his Gucci cologne.

She returned the compliment, stating, "You looking pretty good yourself. I guess you do clean up good. So you going to give me a tour or am I going to have to show myself around?" Inside, Jelisa knew she was playing with fire by flirting with Donny. Shamar would have a whole fit if he caught wind of her antics. But, unfortunately for him, his track record of being there for her was shaky as of late.

Donny nodded, took her by the hand, and led her up the stairs to his master bedroom, which had a sliding glass door that led out to a balcony where she could see the clearest sky she had ever seen. The stars seemed to shine brighter than ever. Unbeknownst to her, Donny had grabbed a bottle of Hennessy on the way up to the room. There was a glass table and two glasses already filled with ice, awaiting their drinks. Donny was calculated, and he knew Jelisa wouldn't be able to

resist coming to see what he had thrown together.
Just before she walked in, from inside the house
Donny saw Jelisa getting out of her car. He was
quick on his feet as he made sure things were in
order when she came in. As she sipped the drink
he poured for her, Donny leaned back against the
rail of the balcony and smiled at her.

"What? Why you looking at me like that?"
Jelisa asked, cracking a smile and blushing.

"Nothing. I'm just wondering what could be
so important that a man would leave a woman
like you alone. I mean, I know dude is in the
military; but he couldn't do nothing to stay
home?" Donny was attempting to plant a seed of
doubt in her heart in hopes that she would seek
comfort in his arms someday.

It wasn't working. Even though the buzz from
her drink was starting to kick in, she quickly
snapped out of it. "What? I don't know about all
that. Where did that come from? Boy, I'm just
trying to have a good time and you blowing my
buzz with all that."

Donny didn't panic. Knowing that his com-
ment rubbed her the wrong way, he quickly
recovered. "Naw, baby girl; it ain't like that.
Didn't mean any disrespect. I'll leave it alone. I
don't want to mess up the mood." He gently ran
his hand across her cheek, and she quickly for-
gave him. The smell of his cologne on his hand

made her forget what she was offended about.

"You good. I just don't like to get into my personal business when I'm chilling, that's all. You got a nice place here. I had no idea it was this nice. Looking at it from the outside, it didn't seem so big. You live here all by yourself?"

Donny liked that she was impressed by his bachelor pad. "Thanks, I try. Yeah, I'm in here solo. You know, maybe one day that special lady will come and make this house into a home. For now, it's me and my son. He spends the weekends with me when he's not with his mother."

Jelisa was more impressed that he was an involved father than she was that he had his own place. She could feel the liquor starting to take a stronger effect on her as she knocked back a second and third drink. Jelisa kept checking the time on her phone trying to make sure she didn't allow herself to stay longer than she should. She set her phone on the table next to her drink and returned her attention to their conversation. As more time went by she could feel herself getting sleepy, as she usually did when she drank too much. Her street sense kicked in and reminded her not to trust even Donny when alcohol was involved. She knew that most men wouldn't hesitate to slip her into the bed and out of her dress in her condition.

"Well, it's getting late. I should probably be getting out of here."

Seeing his opportunity to have her for the night slipping away, Donny protested. "Naw, baby girl, you ain't gotta go nowhere. I'll take you home if you don't feel up to driving."

Not one to be fooled, Jelisa refused. "No, I'm straight. Thanks, though."

"Well, at least let me walk you to your car."

Jelisa nodded in agreement.

Donny walked her to the driver's side of her car, gave her a hug, and watched as she drove off. In his mind, he was satisfied that he at least planted the seed. She may not have given in just yet, but he knew it was only a matter of time. For now, at least the wall she had put up was down. He now had a little more of her trust, and he was patient and persistent enough to wait for his chance.

Jelisa barely made it back home without wrecking her car. She took all of the side streets and stopped at every stop sign completely, trying not to attract any attention to herself. This evening had been just what she needed to get her mind off of the drama with her mother.

When she made it in the apartment, Shawnie and TT were fast asleep on the couch. Mya had also fallen asleep with her head on Shawnie's chest. Jelisa didn't want to wake them, so she quietly went into the back to her room. She showered and changed clothes, and then carefully maneuvered into the kitchen to fix herself a drink. When she dropped a cube of ice on the floor, Shawnie jumped up. She was a light sleeper, and she was so startled that she nearly knocked Mya to the floor, but her reflexes caught her.

"Hey, Lisa, when you get back?" Shawnie asked, clearing her throat and yawning. "Hell, did I fall asleep? My bad, girl. So where did you end up going?"

Jelisa was feeling a lot better after her night out and a nice hot shower. It didn't bother her at all to talk about the day's events. "Girl, you all right. I ended up going over to Donny's house for this kickback he threw together. He was cute." Not even realizing what she had just said, Jelisa didn't have a chance to correct herself when Shawnie's eyebrows arched, and she looked back over the couch.

"Excuse me, what did you just say?" She knew she had heard right; Jelisa had just said that Donny was cute. Although she agreed with her, Jelisa saying it in that context didn't sit right with her.

"What? All I said was I ended up going to Donny's for this little thing he threw together. Then I said it was cute."

Not buying it, Shawnie shook her head and rolled her eyes. "Lisa, please, you said he was cute, not it. Are you still tipsy or something? Please tell me you not messing with this dude."

Jelisa was shocked and offended that Shawnie was coming at her like that. Her face frowned up, and she rolled her eyes, not acknowledging the question. Although she wouldn't admit to it, she knew Shawnie was right. Jelisa was starting to develop feelings for Donny. But for the time being, she would suppress them out of respect for Shamar. "Shawnie, quit playing. If I said that, I didn't mean it. Girl, I'm still buzzed. I need to lie down."

"Yeah, okay, Lisa, go ahead and play with fire, goofy. I hope you not dumb enough to be messing over Shamar while he's deployed. That's dirty as hell."

Jelisa interrupted with a frown on her face. Gritting her teeth and trying not to wake Mya, she replied, "Shawnie, stop it. God! I'm not stupid. I just needed to get out of the house and breathe. I haven't done anything for myself since Shamar left. It's been two months already. If it ain't paying Mama's bills or staying at the shop all day, it's always something. I just needed some time to myself. Ain't nobody thinking about Donny." Jelisa figured the more she denied her feelings for Donny, the better her chances were that they would just go away.

"All right, sis, I'm just saying. I know you and Shamar been through some stuff but y'all belong together, and ain't nothing this side of marriage worth losing that, feel me?"

Jelisa knew she couldn't keep anything from Shawnie because she could usually read between the lines. That's also why she loved Shawnie so much; she always had the right words to say and could make the most complicated things make sense. "I got you, sis, and I appreciate y'all staying over. I miss times like this when we used to stay up all night and talk. But look, I've got a headache and this little bit of juice I just drank has my stomach bubbling. I need to go lie down. Y'all can pull the couch out and sleep on the bed if you want to. Good night now, love you." Jelisa walked off into the dark toward her room.

"All right, honey, I'll see you in the morning. Love you too."

As Jelisa's day was finally ending, Shamar's was just getting started. The mood around the unit was a heavy one. Roll call was at 7:00 a.m.; and, just before breakfast, news came down from command that there had been an attack on one of the supply convoys heading down to Baghdad. This hit home with Shamar because he had just gotten word that Omar was one of the drivers and his vehicle had been struck by an improvised explosive device, what they knew as an IED. The convoy was ambushed just miles from its destination, and Omar's vehicle was caught right in the middle of it. No one in the vehicle survived.

This news crushed Shamar to his core. He was only two months into his tour, and he had already seen death, firsthand, on two occasions. Death itself wasn't new to him; he had buried a number of his homies and put in some work of his own. But losing his boys was just part of being in the streets; you never knew who you could really trust. With Omar, they had gone through so much together. Having to face this tragedy drove him over the edge. They had been tight since basic training and the whole unit knew just how close they were. Over the next few days, Shamar spent a lot of time by himself. He didn't speak about Omar, and his attitude was the worst.

One morning, his commander sent for him to come and meet for breakfast. This was quite unusual, but Shamar knew what it was about.

He arrived at the dining facility where he had been told to meet the commander, Captain Miller. Rank didn't matter to Shamar when it came to authority; he knew how to conduct himself around the higher-ups. It didn't affect him one way or the other.

"Good morning, sir. How are you? " Shamar said, standing at attention next to the table Captain Miller was sitting at.

"Good morning, Sergeant. Take a seat."

As he took his seat, Shamar tried to read the commander's body language. He was six feet two and had to have weighed at least two hundred fifty pounds, all muscle. His deep raspy baritone voice demanded respect and could silence even the toughest soldier. Truth be told, he was actually just like Shamar, a hood dude that used the military to get off the streets before they got him killed.

Captain Miller's demeanor changed when Shamar sat down. "What's good, young bull?" he said in his North Philly accent. "Thanks for coming to talk with me. How you feeling?"

Shamar was caught off guard by his nonchalant demeanor. Never had he felt this comfortable talking to an officer, but there was something about Captain Miller that put Shamar at ease. So he relaxed, still keeping in mind that he was in the presence of his commanding officer.

He prepared his mind and replied, "I'm good, sir, just kind of stressed right now. It seems like everything around me is falling apart. I don't know how much longer I can take this." Shamar shook his head and lowered it in defeat.

"Hold ya head up, li'l bro. I know it gets crazy out here. But this ain't nothing we didn't see in the streets. We both had homies fall. We all took losses; and unless we wanted to join them, the only thing we could do was take the hit and move on, feel me?"

Shamar nodded his head in acknowledgment.

"I think you need to go home and take some time to get yourself together, see about your family. Have you talked to your wife?"

Shamar instantly became anxious. He wasn't prepared to get this personal with his commander, but he felt like he was back home talking to one of the OGs, so the feeling quickly passed. Barely lifting his head, he responded, "No, I haven't. It's been over a week since we last spoke. Every time I think to call, something comes up, and it ends up on the backburner. I don't know, sir. I'm kind of numb to everything. But you're right; I do need to go home for a while. Maybe I'll surprise her."

Captain Miller's faced frowned up when Shamar said that. He sucked his teeth and shook his head.

"What?" Shamar inquired. The look on Captain Miller's face gave the impression that he had said something wrong.

"Li'l homie, that's not something I think you should do. You sure you really wanna open that door? I mean, you said yourself that you haven't spoken to shawty in a while. You don't know what she might be up to. I know that's tough to think about; but, let's be real, women don't tend to fare too well during deployments. Call her first."

Unwilling to admit it, Shamar knew he was right. He had seen countless Army wives do their husbands dirty while they were deployed. Truth be told, he figured something like that was possible, especially with Jelisa staying in the city while he was gone. She was a walking target for thirsty cornballs who just wanted to milk her for her money, and grimy friends who would do the same.

"Yeah, you right. I'll call her. Look, I really appreciate you looking out for me like this, sir. I definitely wasn't expecting this."

Captain Miller grinned and nodded his head. "I got you, homie. I know what it's like. A lot of times, y'all soldiers get overlooked. I can't have one of y'all going crazy on me, feel me? So just let me know when you want to go, and I'll make arrangements for it to happen. But you gotta take care of yourself." Captain Miller stood up, and so did Shamar.

"Thanks, sir," Shamar said as they shook hands and went their separate ways.

Feeling good about the outcome of the meeting, Shamar headed straight to the call center, hoping to catch Jelisa before she went to bed. She was a night owl so calling her at 1:00 a.m. wouldn't be out of the ordinary. He took a deep breath as the phone began to ring. After a few rings, he was just about to hang up when it picked up.

"Hello? Who dis?" a deep voice said.

Shamar took the phone away from his ear and stared at it in disbelief. He had to be trippin'. He returned the phone to his ear and demanded answers. "Yo, who the hell is this and why are you answering my phone?"

The man on the other end sinisterly laughed, toying with him.

"Say, bruh, I don't know who this is but you ain't 'bout that life, so I suggest you put my wife on the phone before things get real ugly, feel me?"

The man on the other end laughed again. "She busy, bruh." Then the man hung up on him.

Shamar, now furious, immediately called back; but this time it went straight to voice mail. After five failed attempts, Shamar gave up and called Sandra, hoping that she would give him some answers. She didn't pick up either; her phone too went straight to voice mail. He didn't want to leave a message and was now hit with anxiety and rage. He didn't know if Jelisa was in trouble or if she was dumb enough to be creeping and leave her phone unattended. Either way, he was going to be on the first flight home. He needed answers, and things had just gotten real. Hopefully, this wouldn't end up bad.

Shamar left a message at headquarters for Captain Miller, informing him that he wanted to go home on R&R with the next group. That would give him just two days before he could go home and he hoped to have some answers before then. He at least wanted to know what he was going home to before he got there. Determined not to let this get to him, he went back to work in an effort to keep himself busy.

While Shamar was going crazy over the phone incident, Jelisa was fast asleep at home. Her day had been so busy and draining that she hadn't even noticed that she had left her phone at Donny's on the balcony when she rushed out.

It wasn't until two o'clock the next morning that she was awakened out of her sleep with the urge to use the bathroom when she realized she couldn't find her phone. It was too late to go to the shop to see if she left it there, so she logged on to her computer and pulled up her phone company's Web site to track her phone. She couldn't believe what she was reading. Her eyes got big as the address of the location of her phone wasn't the shop's address; it was Donny's.

"What the hell is this goofy doing with my phone and why wouldn't he bring it to me?" Jelisa questioned herself. The more she thought about it, she was overcome with concern. What if Shamar called? Would Donny be that disrespectful that he'd play on her phone? She knew some guys who would have taken full advantage of something like that.

"Shamar is going to flip! God, please don't let this man have answered my phone," she pleaded under her breath.

Jelisa had to force herself to fall back asleep because of the thought of the possible backlash. When the morning came, she dropped Mya off to Shawnie for her to keep her for the day, then she headed to the shop. It was Saturday, so it was the busiest day of the week for her. But the only thing on her mind was cussing Donny out for not telling her he had her phone.

When she arrived at the shop, her attitude was in full effect. Lo and behold, her phone was in the drawer at her workstation, right where she thought she'd left it. She looked at Donny, ready to crack the side of his head open with her blow dryer. Donny glanced over at her; he could tell she wanted to say something.

"What's good, baby girl? Why you looking at me like that?"

"Donny, wipe that stupid look off of your face and stop playing with me. What were you doing with my phone last night?"

Donny tried keeping a straight face while denying it but Jelisa wasn't having it. "Hey, shorty, I don't know what you talking about."

"Yeah, I bet," she snapped back. "Donny, you wrong as hell for that. I tracked my phone with GPS last night, and it came up at your address. I don't know what you thought was funny about that, but you better not have been playing on my phone."

Donny's head was bowed as he continued cutting his client's hair. He looked up innocently with a partial smirk. "Shawty, I don't know what you talking about."

As much as she wanted to pop off, it was the beginning of her day, and she didn't want her whole day to be ruined by Donny's little stunt.

She shook it off and went on about her day. She only hoped that Donny hadn't done anything stupid with her phone that she would have to pay for later. She scrolled through her phone and didn't see any missed calls or messages, so she believed she was in the clear.

On Monday morning, Shamar got a message from Captain Miller that he was slotted to be on the next plane heading back to the States for R&R. He was given two weeks to go home and make things right with Jelisa. He hadn't spoken to her in almost two weeks now, and he had begun to wonder if she would even want to speak to him. Shamar was still conflicted about what had happened to Omar, and he wasn't prepared to talk to anyone about it, not even Jelisa. Anxiety and worry filled his heart as he boarded the plane leaving Kuwait International Airport.

When he landed in Chicago, he was met by the freezing November winds coming off of the lakefront. He didn't tell Jelisa he was coming and he hoped that his suspicions were wrong. All he could think about as the bus from the airport pulled into the city was finding the identity of the man who answered her phone. Shamar was tormenting himself with thoughts of her cheating, having some dude off spending his money and making him look like a fool. The more he thought about it, the angrier he became.

Waiting at the bus drop-off was a black Yukon XL with blacked-out tint and blunt smoke seeping out the partially cracked windows. The bass coming from the back of the SUV made the windows at the nearby gas station rattle. From the driver's side appeared Kaduwey Jones, a six foot two inch brown-skinned goon with dreads down to his shoulders, Versace sunglasses, and a gold grill in his mouth. With a blunt hanging from his mouth and a cell phone and keys in his hands, Shamar's best friend greeted him with some dap and a big grin, showing off his golden smile.

"What's happenin', my G?" Kaduwey said with his Midwest accent, which sounded more Southern that anything. Kaduwey was Shamar's best friend before he went off to the Army. The two were inseparable whenever they reunited. The last time the two had seen each other was just before Shamar shipped off to Germany. They spoke on the phone whenever he went home on leave, but they always seemed to miss seeing each other. The years had gone by fast, but it was as if they didn't even miss a beat.

"What up, homie? You killin' 'em, ain't you? Thanks for coming through for me, bruh."

Kaduwey took a pull from his blunt and looked from Shamar to the twenty-eight-inch rims that shined in the sunlight. "You know me, folk. I gets it in; you know how I do. Thirty-four! Let's go, man. Get in; we drawing too much attention out here. You know them boys be watching."

"Thirty-four" stood for the highway exit that led to Michigan City from I-94. Exit 34B was a movement in the city, and anybody who was somebody repped it hard. They both laughed as they got into the smoked-out SUV and whipped out of the parking lot, heading down Franklin Street back toward the highway.

"Where we going, fam? I thought you was taking me to the crib."

Kaduwey looked over at Shamar as if he had forgotten who he was talking to. "Folk, for real? What, you just going to walk around the city in your Army uniform like it's hot or something?"

Shamar looked down at his uniform and shook his head. He'd totally forgotten that he didn't have a chance to pack any civilian clothing when he was first deployed, so he had to travel in what he had. "Man, I don't know what I was thinking. Take me to the Village so I can grab a couple 'fits."

Kaduwey and Shamar thought alike, and that was why they got along so well. In the fifteen years they'd known each other, there was never a fight or disagreement between them. Kaduwey smoked that last piece of his blunt and tossed it out the window. He blew out a cloud of smoke and turned to Shamar with a serious look on his face.

"Hey, what's good, homie? Why you looking at me like that? Go on and spill it; I know you got something to say." Shamar laughed. He could always tell when his partner in crime had something on his mind. He would get quiet and have this blank look on his face like he was in deep thought.

"Yeah, folk, you know me; I'm always thinking. What's up with Chrissy?"

The sound of that name made Shamar's heart thunder with anger and anxiety. The grin on his face from being home was quickly replaced by a cold stare. "Really, fam? I just came home and you already hitting me with this? No, I haven't talked to that goofy. She still denying everything and I'm stuck, 'cause if I say anything, all hell's going to break loose. You know how this city is; word get out about something like that and the whole town will be buzzing."

Chrissy was an old high school fling Shamar had been messing with around the time he had first started talking to Jelisa. They had actually met while he was in the group home briefly when his mother passed. She was three years his senior, and she had a thing for young hustlers. They met again when she moved to Michigan City from Chicago. Shamar had already been given the heads-up by one of her homegirls that she was feeling him. Hearing that intensified the crush he had already had on her; he just had to have her.

"Hey, why did you bring her up?"

"Folk, I keep telling you that you better deal with that before it comes to deal with you. You know the truth and you know what I always say: 'the truth don't need no support and a lie don't care who tells it.'"

Shamar had to admit that he had a point. At the time that Chrissy and Shamar hooked up, she was already stuck in a worthless relationship with some goofy white boy who was infatuated with black girls. Chrissy, however, was half black and half white. Since the child she had already had was white, no one would have guessed that when she popped up pregnant just weeks after she and Shamar slept together, the pale-skinned baby might have been his.

"Hey, I don't even know what to think right now. If I go after her about it and I'm wrong, my family name is burnt out here, and her marriage is over."

Kaduwey had a disgusted look on his face while having to listen to Shamar sidestep the issue with his compassion for Chrissy and her family. "Yo, for real, Shamar, the Army done made you hella soft. Since when did you start worrying about these bust downs? I'm just saying don't let that ho play you for no sucka. I don't care how light-skinned that little girl is, she look just like Mya. You always did like those crazy broads, but I can see you ain't up to dealing with it. But I'm telling you, folk, you better deal with it before it's too late," he warned him.

For a moment Shamar found himself reliving the time he met Chrissy. It was still vivid in his mind.

In the Chi

Shamar made it to the corner of the block, highly irritated after the argument with Mrs. Turner, or "the old bag" as he put it. He stopped near a street sign to spark up the blunt he had rolled. With nothing actually planned for the day he continued walking and smoking, waiting for his buzz to kick in. The fall air had a slight sting to it and was cooler than usual that Friday morning.

Shamar made it to his usual hangout spot: a park just a few blocks from the group home. He never walked farther than four or five blocks. He always made sure if he ran into trouble he wouldn't have to run that far. Sitting on the edge of a picnic table Shamar continued to medicate, occasionally choking on the smoke. He dug around in his pocket and pulled out the bracelet. Man, Joe, I wonder what she doing right now? I can't believe it's been this long. I wonder if she still remembers me, *Shamar wondered about his mother in heaven. He didn't know if she could but, if so, did she even think about him as much as he did her?*

"Who is this fool here?" Shamar said under his breath. He noticed an image walking toward him from the other side of the park. He looked around, quickly taking note of every escape route just in case this stranger was a stick-up kid. Shamar tensed up when he ran his hand across his waist and realized he didn't strap up. "God," he mumbled.

As the image got closer, his heart pounded rapidly, and adrenaline started pumping. Suddenly the image, who turned out to be a young female, reached her hand in her pants pocket. He slowly slid off the table. In the Chi you never know what was up with people;

*females would jack you and set you up just as
quickly as niggas would.* I should have worn
my contacts. I can't see for nothing. Who is that?
Just my luck I would be the one today, *Shamar
said to himself.*

The female's hand appeared out of her pocket,
and she began to raise it. Just when he was
about to make a quick dash she called out,
"Shamar, what's up, boo? Why did I just have
a whole argument with these Arabs at the gas
station over some stupid Cheetos? I was about
to cut one of them goofies."

Shamar let out a huge sigh when he realized
it was his homegirl Chrissy. She kept rambling
on and on until she noticed him staring at her in
a daze. He couldn't believe he let her spook him
like that.

"Dang, boy, snap out of it. You staring hella
hard right now. Why is you looking at me like
that?" she asked.

"Oh, my bad, Chrissy. I didn't know who you
was coming over here. I was about to get ghost
on you real fast, Joe. You lucky I left the Tre at
the crib," he joked as he stood up all the way
and began walking toward her with his hands
open for a hug.

"Yeah, right, nigga. You lucky 'cause I would
have cut yo' ass before you had the chance
to take that little raggedy burner off safety,"

Chrissy replied, meeting his gesture for a hug. After they had separated, the two walked back over to the picnic table and sat down.

Now Chrissy was a live one for real. Her five foot four frame and squeaky voice were deceiving to the unsuspecting Opp. It didn't take much to set her off, and not even her crush on Shamar was enough to calm her down if he was there when somebody set her off. "What's up with you, girl? Where you say you were coming from again? I'm sorry them jeans kind of caught me off guard," he said, licking his lips and giving her the once over.

"Boy, you stupid. I said I just came from the gas station messing with them Arabs. You know how they are. Stupid woman told me I was trying to steal some funky bag of Cheetos. What I look like?" she said, smirking with an attitude.

Chrissy liked to pick with the Arabs at the gas stations and corner stores. She always thought it was funny to see them get mad and try to chase people out. Shamar always had a thing for her, but sometimes she was way too childish for him. He figured out awhile ago that she liked him; but she was nineteen then and, to him, it wasn't worth it to get involved with someone who was so unpredictable.

He responded, "Chrissy, you play too much. Keep on messing with them folks and they gon' get you one of these days. What you do this time? Walking around eating those chips before you paid for them, weren't you?"

Chrissy smiled and nodded in agreement. "Let me hit that," she said, nodding her head toward the half-smoked blunt in his hand.

Shamar took a puff and handed it over to her. He watched as she licked her thick, glossy lips before wrapping them around the tip of the blunt. Looking her up and down, he traced her curves with his eyes, wishing that she weren't so young minded. She thick as hell. *He then teased her, saying, "Chrissy, you sexy as hell, you know that?"*

She choked on the weed smoke, caught off guard by his version of a compliment. "Boy, shut up! You play too much," she snapped back playfully.

Shamar grinned and laughed. "What? I ain't playing."

"Then why you ain't cuff me yet? You know I'm a rider, and I got that," she said as she bit her bottom lip and started twerking on the edge of the table. It drove him crazy.

"'Cause you too high-strung, Chrissy. I can't take you nowhere. You always trying to fight somebody," he answered.

She knew Shamar was right and she hated that he teased her like he did. She would do anything for him, and no one could ever say anything bad to her about him. She was his little bad chick, and they had history.

She was quiet back then, but one day while Shamar was out two boys cornered her and tried taking what they thought she was flaunting. Chrissy, already tired of them picking on her, caught one of them slipping. While he was trying to rip her skirt off, she slipped a razor from under her tongue and sliced the side of his face up. Just as the other one tried to move in on her Shamar showed up.

Without hesitation, he jumped in and put the beats on him. Because of that, Mrs. Turner and the social worker were ready to throw baby girl out for using violence, but Shamar managed to sweet talk Mrs. Turner and explain everything. From that point on, Chrissy's loyalty lay with him and, after going back home with her mother, she still came to see him almost every day.

Chrissy moved closer to Shamar, put her hand on the inside of his thigh, and blew weed smoke at his crotch. She looked up at him seductively and said, "I know I'm a little crazy, but you're the only one who can tame me."

She licked her lips and took another hit and Shamar caressed her cheek, gazing back into her eyes. Then he leaned down until their foreheads met and said, "Girl, give me back my weed. You trippin'! I was just messing with you, goofy. Stop playing."

Chrissy leaned back up with a disappointed look on her face.

"Aww, poor baby. You mad now?" Shamar teased, knowing that he really wanted her to wrap those juicy lips around something else.

"I can't stand you boy, ugh!" she said.

Shamar snickered and finished off what was left of the blunt, and before he knew it he got the munchies. "Come to the corner store with me real quick. I'm hella hungry," he said, hopping off the table.

Chrissy followed suit. "All right. Can you buy me a soda?"

"Yeah, a soda . . . pop!" he said, smacking her butt as she walked in front of him.

"Boy, you better stop. You know I like that stuff." Chrissy laughed.

The two headed back across the park to the main road toward the nearest corner store. Chrissy had completely taken Shamar's mind off of everything that had transpired earlier.

*Things were good, and he hoped they would
stay that way. However, they wouldn't. After a
night alone with each other, out of nowhere one
of Shamar's uncles came to pick him up and it
would be years before they saw each other again.*

After hitting the mall for some gear, Kaduwey
and Shamar headed back to the city to catch
up with the homies on the south side. Jelisa
was enjoying her day off since the shop was
unusually closed this Monday. The only thing
she could think about was the fact that Shamar
hadn't called at all. The reports on the news
were talking about soldiers who had been killed,
and she prayed that she never got that kind of
call. She hadn't spoken to her mother but once
since their fallout, and that was only because
Shawnie made them talk.

Later that evening, all of the sisters were at
Sandra's house having dinner when Shawnie
heard a light knock on the door. Jelisa was standing in the living room, talking to TT. The house
was loud and the combination of the TV and
stereo playing drowned out the conversation.
When Shawnie opened the door, Shamar stood
before her, motioning with his finger over his
mouth for her not to say anything. He gave her a

quick hug and slowly crept up behind Jelisa, who was a couple shots in and fully distracted by her conversation. Everybody grew slight smiles on their faces as Shamar inched closer to her. He gently wrapped his arm around her waist and kissed her on her neck.

"What the hell?" she said as she spun around and jumped back. Seeing Shamar standing there left her speechless and tears flooded her eyes. She couldn't believe he was actually there.

Jelisa experienced a rollercoaster of emotions as she embraced Shamar. The past couple of months had taken her to places within the depths of her heart that she never knew existed. She didn't want this moment to end. As Shamar wiped the tears from her face, she was reminded why she fell in love with him in the beginning; he was her protector and her lover. Seeing him made her forget that she hadn't heard from him in so long. Her mind reasoned that it was to build up the anticipation for his surprise return.

"You know I missed you, right?" Shamar said, helping her to the couch. He quickly gave everyone hugs and sat down next to her.

Jelisa nodded, still wiping the tears away. "Why didn't you tell me you were coming home? I was so mad at you for not calling me. You don't know what I've been through without you here."

Not wanting to let the moment be spoiled by complaining, Jelisa tried her best to calm down.

"I know, love; and I wish I could have been here for you. There's a reason why I haven't called, but we'll talk about that later. I just want to spend some time with y'all. I've got two weeks before I have to go back so let's just enjoy it." Shamar's attempt to put her at ease was working; and they spent the rest of the night laughing, joking, and catching up.

Once Mya was put to bed, Jelisa and Shamar headed back to her apartment to spend some time alone. Jelisa knew it would be hard for her to keep him to herself for the whole time he was home.

Shamar was impressed with the way Jelisa had the place decorated. "You did good, honey. I like what you did to the place. What you got to drink up in here?"

Shamar made his way around the apartment, giving himself a tour. He noticed there were no pictures of him anywhere in the apartment, which made him feel a bit slighted, especially with her supposedly missing him so much. He shook it off and joined her at the kitchen table, where she had poured two glasses of E&J.

Jelisa, thumbing through her phone, felt Shamar looking at her. "What? Why you looking at me like that?" she asked.

Shamar was staring off into the space behind her. "Oh, my bad. I'm just thinking, wishing I didn't have to go back. I miss regular life, just being able to do normal stuff. Know what I'm saying?"

"Yeah, I know what you mean. I think about that sometimes too. But how was it over there? Is it as bad as they say it is on the news?" Jelisa asked, placing her hand on his knee. "I mean, you would tell me if something was going on with you, wouldn't you? I hear about all of these soldiers coming back after seeing so much over there, and they aren't the same anymore. I just—"

Shamar cut her off before she could finish. "I know where you're going with this and I'm telling you I'm straight. Don't worry about me. I haven't seen nothing over there that I hadn't already seen out here on these streets. Anyway, what's really been up with you?" he said, pointing at her freshly done hair and the red bottom heels she was wearing. "Is this what you've been spending all my money on?"

Jelisa couldn't tell if he was serious or just messing with her, so she brushed it off. "Boy, please. I got my own money. Quit playing. Besides, you know I'm wearing the hell out of these heels. It's all for you, Daddy," she whispered seductively in his ear as she slowly stood up and walked past him, purposely swaying her hips to show him what he'd been missing out on.

Jelisa walked over to the sink and began rinsing off the few dishes that were still there from earlier. Shamar slipped off his Pelle Pelle coat and pulled his white tee over his head, revealing his rock-hard abs hidden under a wife beater. While the shirt covered his head, Jelisa glanced over her shoulder just in time to see his accidental strip tease and she immediately got moist. The sight of Shamar standing there in that wife beater, jeans, and brand new Jordans reminded her of the first time they met.

He walked over to her, wrapping his arms around her waist as she poked her butt out, welcoming him to come closer. He leaned in and kissed her on her neck, making her knees nearly give out on her. Shamar received no resistance as he took her right there in the kitchen. He picked her up by her waist as she wrapped her legs around his and her hands held on to the back of his neck. He spun around and laid her on the table and feasted on every part of her. They rekindled their love for each other for the next two hours; and, by midnight, the bottle of E&J was empty, and they were fast asleep in the living room on the couch.

As her body lay on top of his, she was suddenly awakened by the twitching of his muscles. Jelisa looked at Shamar's face, and she could see his eyes racing back and forth behind his eyelids. He moaned and groaned in anguish. Whatever he was dreaming about was tormenting him, and she had to wake him.

Patting him on his chest gently so as not to startle him, she called out to him, "Babe, babe. Shamar, wake up." He wouldn't budge. She rubbed her hand on the side of his face, calling his name out louder. "Shamar, please wake up! Wake up!"

Suddenly, his eyes sprang open and, without warning, he grabbed her by the throat, flipping them both off of the couch and onto the floor. Jelisa struggled for air, kicking and clawing away at his chest while begging him to let go. There was a deadness in his eyes and, as she could feel the life escaping her, she reached over to the coffee table and grabbed the empty E&J bottle, smashing it across Shamar's head. He blacked out; and when he came to, he awoke to a terrified Jelisa trembling in the corner, naked and wrapped up in a blanket.

Shamar's head was pounding and he felt dizzy. He had no idea what had just happened. The last thing he could remember was falling asleep on the couch. The next thing he knew, he was dodging bullets in Iraq. "Baby, what's wrong? Jelisa, why is there glass all over the place?" He tried getting up but was quickly knocked back down by gravity and the huge headache he now had.

Jelisa didn't reply; she stayed in the corner, shaking her head and crying. "Stay away from me!" she cried out.

Shamar stood up, put his boxers on, and cautiously approached Jelisa. "Jelisa, please tell me what happened. Why are you crying? What did I do?"

For a second she couldn't believe he was even asking this question, but the look on his face told her that he genuinely had no idea what had just happened. "You . . . you choked me. I was just trying to wake you up, and you choked me," she said as she continued to cry.

Shamar reached out to her, and she shrank back farther into the corner. "Baby, come here. I swear I won't hurt you. I can't even remember what happened. You've got to believe me." Shamar helped her to her feet and walked her over to the couch that they were lying on before he tried to choke the life out of her. He wrapped his arms around her as they huddled underneath the cover.

"Jelisa, I am so sorry. I swear I don't know
what happened. You know I would never put
my hands on you, or any other woman. You
believe me, right?" Shamar pleaded with her to
forgive him. He searched his mind, looking for
an explanation of what had just taken place.

"I can't do this right now. The person I just
saw with his hands around my throat was a
totally different person. I don't know who you
are anymore. Please just leave me alone." Jelisa
pulled the cover off of her and got up. She went
to her room, locking the door behind her, and
cried herself to sleep, confused about what had
taken place. What would have happened if she
hadn't been able to get him off of her?

Shamar remained sitting on the couch with
his face in his hands, trying to understand what
came over him. He eventually fell asleep on the
couch around 5:00 a.m. but was awakened by an
eerie feeling that somebody was watching him.
As he came to, Jelisa sat in a nearby recliner,
partially hidden under a blanket. She sat silently
drinking a cup of tea, trying to nurse her bruised
and sore throat.

Sitting up, Shamar cleared his throat and
greeted his weakened wife. "Hey, Jelisa, how
you doing? Listen, I'm sorry for what happened
last night."

Jelisa remained quiet.

"I honestly don't know what came over me. I wish I could explain it, but I promise it won't happen again."

Jelisa rolled her eyes and took a sip of her tea. "Shamar, you can't promise that. You didn't even know you were capable of doing that to me. What happened to you over there that has scarred you so much? You are a completely different person, Shamar, and I'm scared. How do I know you won't wake up one day and hurt me again? Worse yet, hurt Mya."

Shamar bowed his head in shame. He had heard about this happening to the white boys he served with but never a brother. Being from the hood and seeing the things he'd seen coming up, it never crossed his mind that it could be him. He knew what it was, but his pride wouldn't let him admit that he was that weak-minded. "Jelisa, can we talk about this another time?" Shamar asked, attempting to dismiss her line of questions.

"No, we can't, Shamar. We're going to deal with this right now. I went online and saw that there's something called PTSD. I think you need to talk to somebody."

Shamar could have sworn she was reading his mind when she said that. "Babe, don't do this. I'm not crazy. I don't need no shrink to tell me how I'm feeling. I told you I'm good. Can we not do this right now? I just want to make sure you're okay. I just need to get used to being back. It's all foreign to me, that's all. I'll be okay, I promise."

Rubbing her throat, Jelisa gave Shamar a dissatisfied look. "I hear you, Shamar. At least go talk to my dad because this here, you acting like you can't talk to me, is not going to work. I'm gonna need you to handle that today, and I am so serious." Jelisa got up and went to go shower, leaving Shamar to consider her warning.

He knew she was serious and it would mean that the next two weeks were not going to be good at all. He didn't mind talking with Pete; he, of all people, would understand, having gone to Vietnam and come back to deal with stubborn women like Jelisa.

After getting himself together for the day, Shamar called Kaduwey to go and pick up something to drive while he was in town. It didn't feel quite like home without his own set of wheels to push around. Around noon, Kaduwey came through to pick Shamar up; you could hear the thunder of his speakers from two blocks away.

Like clockwork, Shamar walked outside just as he was pulling up. "Ay, what's good, my dude?" Kaduwey greeted Shamar with smoke coming from his nose and mouth.

"What's good with it, folk? Bruh, it ain't even one o'clock yet and you blowing purp already? You better hope they don't piss me when I get back 'cause I'm gonna pop up hot just off contact, messing with you."

Kaduwey grinned with his fourteen-karat smile and his eyes barely open. "I'm good, G; you know me. Hell, you look like you need a blunt or two. You wanna hit this? What happened to you?" he questioned. It wasn't hard to read Shamar. You could fit a week's worth of luggage in the bags under his eyes.

"Hey, I don't know what's going on with me, man. I spazzed out on Jelisa last night, and I swear I can't remember none of it."

Kaduwey was confused; he had never known Shamar to put his hands on any female. He had too much self-control for that, so he knew something had to be wrong. "Man, that ain't even you."

As they navigated through traffic, they ended up on Walker at one of Kaduwey's traps. He put the SUV in park and turned the music down to revisit the topic. Looking over at Shamar, he took one last pull from what was left of the blunt he was smoking and addressed him with sincerity. "Ay, folk, I'ma tell you this, real talk: don't let that war change you, homie. You got a family to look out for.

So, whatever you saw over there, don't let it mess with your head. I can't say I know how it feels, but you remember when we put that work in back in the day. I had nightmares about it. Hell, it screwed with my head, dawg. Now I'm looking over my shoulders every five minutes, and I stay high to calm my nerves."

What Kaduwey was saying must have been getting to Shamar because tears began dancing at the rims of his eyelids. Kaduwey noticed him wipe away a tear and he tapped him on his arm with the back of his hand. "Bruh, what you see over there? I ain't never seen you shed tears unless it involved somebody dying. What happened?"

Chapter Ten

Back to business

After walking and talking for a while Block and Bria ended up back at the park where Toya was just pulling up. It had done Block some good having the opportunity to catch up with Bria; he was starting to feel at home. Not wanting to interrupt, Toya chose to stay in the car to wait for him to finish up. She smiled and kindly waved at Bria through the windshield.

"Well, shawty, I have to say it was real good seeing you. Seriously, I haven't seen a smile as bright as yours in a minute and this really made my day. I'm glad to be home. We should get together later on. Feel me?" Block said, taking her hand into his.

"Yeah, that would be nice, and it was good seeing you again. I really missed you all these years, so we definitely need to catch up," she said seductively. Surprisingly, Block didn't pick up on the fact that she was hitting on him. "Well, here, take my number real quick."

Block was dumbfounded; he didn't have a cell phone nor did he have anything to write with. "Hold on for a minute," he said, slightly jogging over to Toya's car to get paper and a pen. After getting her number, Block bid Bria farewell. "All right, sweetheart. I'm definitely going to holla at you later, all right? Take care now," he said, giving her a warm hug and hesitating for a minute before letting go.

When Block got back into the car, Toya was all jokes. "I'm saying, Block, you ain't waste no time, did you? Get it, boy," Toya teased. "Anyway, we need to get you right before you go see the family. I can't have you coming home looking like this," she said, pointing at his clothes.

"For real, Toya, that's how you gonna play me? What's wrong with how I look? This is me now," Block answered, slightly offended.

As they pulled off, Toya headed toward the east side's Potowatomi Park area. This unincorporated part of town used to be exclusively whites only. Any black family who even ventured to build or buy within its city limits was burned or bullied out. That was, until Block's grandfather came into the picture. After being refused the opportunity to buy his first home there, he was determined to make life hell for every white family living there. After the settlement, empowered by millions of dollars and a highly paid attorney, Grandpa Roland bought up five properties. The Foster family name became solidified from that point on as a force to be reckoned with.

As they turned into the subdivision where the family's properties were located, Block was overcome with amazement at how much things had changed since he'd been gone. He was also feeling anxious as he had never been this far into Potowatomi before. The last he'd heard they were still trying to chase black folk out. The Foster family owned an entire cul-de-sac, and the first house Toya stopped at was immaculate. It was a three-story tan brick house the size of a mini-mansion, with five bedrooms and three baths, and a full basement with a large glass door that opened to a huge backyard.

"What we doing here, Toya? I thought you was taking me to get my gear straight. Whose house is this?" Block inquired, wondering what his sister was up to. He hated surprises; and, after Toya had gotten on him about his appearance, he hoped this wasn't some get-together she was bringing him to.

"Come on, boy," Toya said, turning the car off and unbuckling her seat belt.

"I don't know, Toya. You know they don't like black folk out here. I ain't trying to have the Klan after me my first day out," Block commented, only partially joking.

As the two of them stood in the middle of the street, Block looked around, surveying and admiring the architecture. "So what's up, sis? Don't leave me in suspense. This supposed to be some kind of joke or something?" he asked.

"Naw, bro, this is you," Toya replied.

Block's face had confusion written all over it. "What you mean this me? Do you see where we at? I'm not trying to buy nothing out here."

Toya smiled and pulled out a set of house keys from her Coach wristlet. As she dangled the keys in his face, she said proudly, "Baby brother, a lot has changed since you left. We run this city. I told you we're in business and there's nobody who can stop us 'cause everything is legal, bro." Toya was getting excited the more detail she gave Block. "Go on and check it out," she said, pointing to the front door of the house.

"Man, sis, you really know how to make a statement. Let's see what we have here," Block said, turning the key and opening the door.

As they walked into the elegant mini-mansion, Block's eyes grew as big as gold balls as he stood in amazement. After all that time behind those walls, this was the last thing he imagined he would come home to. The house was fully furnished with custom wood furniture. The floors were marble, and a huge family portrait was on the wall in the great room.

"So what do you think, baby bro? Ain't this a sight to come home to? One thing, though, you're gonna have to lose those Dickies and wife beaters. That's not the image we're portraying in this family. So go check in the master bedroom closet. I'm pretty sure I got the sizes right," Toya said as she led Block down the hallway.

He stopped in his tracks and stared at the wall behind Toya and commented, "I don't know about all that, Toya. That suit life ain't me, you know what I'm saying?"

"Boy, what you mean you ain't about that life? You ain't no gangsta. That ain't in your blood. You better go on somewhere with that," Toya said sternly.

If there was one thing Block knew it was that he wasn't a different man from when he first went in. Apparently, his big sis had no clue of the kind of person he had to become in order to survive in prison for fifteen years. Those years locked down hardened his heart, and although he'd never make it known to his family, he was indeed a gangsta. Not wanting to open himself up for a deep discussion Block held his tongue and simply answered, "I feel you, sis, but you have no idea; but, since you held me down and you seem to have things in order, I'll roll with it for now."

Toya smiled and nodded, saying, "All right then. Go ahead and get yourself cleaned up and let's go make some moves. As a matter of fact, take your time. I'm sure there are some things you need to take care of first. I don't want to overwhelm you. Look on the dresser in the room. There's a cell phone and car keys. When you're ready, meet me at my condo. Here's my address." She grabbed a pen and pad off a nearby table and wrote down her address.

"All right then, sis, I got you. Look, I appreciate all of this; and, you're right, I do need to handle a few things before I get bogged down by everybody. Give me a hug. I'll hit you up in a few. Love you," Block said.

They embraced, and he walked her out to her car. "I love you, bro. Now go get yourself together. I got something else planned for you tonight. Call me," she said before she got into her car and drove off.

Chapter Eleven

Jelisa called Shawnie to come over and help her figure out what to do after the incident with Shamar. She hadn't been able to go outside all day. She needed to understand how he was capable of hurting her that way, especially considering the years of her life that she'd invested with him. After all of the fistfights and shootouts, the late nights waiting up wondering if he would be coming home or if she would get that godforsaken call, those things now paled in comparison to the pain she felt. Things would never be the same again.

A knock on the door came just as Jelisa passed by it. "Who is it?" she called out, thinking that if it was Shawnie, she should have been using the key she'd given her.

Just as she reached for the lock, her cell phone rang. It was her mother calling. "Hello? Hey, Mama," she said, opening the door. She froze at the sight before her, dropping the phone on the floor.

In the doorway stood a six foot three inch dark-skinned man with a scar on the left side of his face. He had long dreads pouring from under a Kangol hat. The man stood there with a smirk on his face, flashing pearly white teeth with a single gold tooth. His dark eyes pierced through her as she remained stunned and silent, unable to move.

"Well, I see you've grown up to be quite a lovely lady." The dark visitor spoke with a raspy voice that made her shudder.

"What are you doing here and how the hell did you find me?" Jelisa snapped, finally recovering from the shock.

"Well, that's not nice, young lady. You going to invite me in or am I going to have to stand out here in this cold?"

Jelisa's hands starting shaking and rage began to fill every inch of her body. "Reggie, you have a lot of nerve coming here!" she asserted, pointing her finger in his face. "No, the hell you're not welcome in my house; and, yes, the hell you are going to stand out there in the freezing cold. I don't want you anywhere near me, ever!" Jelisa was furious. The thought of the man who raped her and literally destroyed her life having the audacity to show up at her door had her beside herself. The last she'd heard, Reggie was in New York somewhere on the run from the feds after a botched bank robbery.

"All right, all right, sweetheart, don't get your panties in a bunch. Old Reggie just wanted to come by and say hi to an old friend, that's all. No need to get all worked up. You act like you don't remember me."

Right then, it all began to make sense. When he spoke those words, Jelisa remembered the strange phone calls she had received months ago. It had been Reggie calling her the whole time. Jelisa's anger turned to anxiety, and his impromptu visit had lasted long enough. "Reggie, I don't have anything to say to you. We don't have any business. There is nothing to talk about. You need to get the hell off my stoop right now and never come here again. You hear me? And I know that was you calling me, too. I swear to God if you ever—"

Reggie took a step closer, cutting her off before she could finish her sentence. "Hey now, baby girl, calm your pretty little self down. I'll be on my way. We'll see each other again real soon." Reggie turned and walked away before she could respond. He jumped into a black Cadillac and sped away.

Jelisa slammed the door and went and poured herself a drink. Moments later, there was another knock at the door, along with the sound of keys jiggling. She looked nervously at the front door, unsure if Reggie had returned or if Shawnie had finally shown up. The doorknob turned, and the door flew open, blown by the wind, followed by the tapping of little footsteps. Mya ran in, jumping into Jelisa's arms as Shawnie struggled to get her keys out of the door.

"Hey, girl, what's up? Sorry I'm late, but those fools out there cannot drive," Shawnie joked.

Jelisa found nothing funny. She stood with her hand on her hip, rolling her eyes.

"What?" Shawnie asked, slightly bothered by Jelisa's stance.

"For real, Shawnie? You could have called or something."

Shawnie snapped back, "First of all, who are you talking to? You better take some of that bass out of your voice, goofy. Second of all, I did call you from Mama's phone, and you hung up on me. Anyways, what's wrong with you?"

Jelisa took the rest of the glass of vodka she was drinking to the head and sent Mya to her room to watch TV. "Girl, I'm sorry. I'm stressing right now. Come in the living room. We have to talk. So, first, you know Shamar and I left

Mama's house last night so we could spend some time alone, right?"

Shawnie grinned. "Yeah, don't I know it? I see he helped you sweat that wrap out."

Jelisa gave a partial smile, still feeling uncomfortable about the situation. "Whatever. Anyway, so after he put it on me, we fell asleep on the couch. The next thing I know, I'm lying on top of him, trying to wake him up, and he freaks out on me. Girl, this fool blacked out and choked the mess out of me. I had to smash a liquor bottle on his head to make him snap out of it."

"Are you serious? That's crazy," Shawnie said in disbelief. She would never put it past Shamar but never in a million years would she have expected him to put his hands on her sister. "So what happened after that? Where is he now?"

"Girl, I don't know. He probably running around somewhere with Kaduwey. Honestly, I don't even care right now. Anyway, that's only half of what happened. You ain't going to believe this. Tell me why this bastard Reggie just popped up at my door."

Shawnie was puzzled. "Reggie? Reggie who? Mama's ex-boyfriend Reggie?"

"Girl, yes. This is some straight Fly Betty type drama. I can't believe he had the nerve to come to my house, of all places, after what he did to me.

Shawnie, I wanted to kill him right there on my stoop."

Shawnie lowered and shook her head. "What did he say? After all this time, why would he come here?"

"Shawnie, I have no idea; but I made it perfectly clear that I never wanted to see him again. I've got way too much going on right now. This mess with Shamar is killing me. I think he saw something over there that he doesn't want to tell me about and it's messing with his head. Whatever it is, I don't like it, and it scares me. He scares me."

"Well, sis, I know it can't be easy for either of you to go through a deployment. Did you tell him to talk to Daddy? You know they get along. Maybe he can help Shamar figure out how to deal with whatever it is because, as sure as he is a man, his pride is not going to let him get professional help."

It always helped Jelisa when she talked to Shawnie. No matter what it was, she had either gone through it or she knew someone who did. Either way, she always had the right words. "Yeah, I told him that it was a deal breaker if he didn't. I need to know that my baby is okay. I can't stand to see him like this. I almost lost him to these streets. Shawnie, I don't want to lose him to this war, no matter if it's in Iraq or just in his mind."

"Yeah, I know, but y'all are meant to be together. Both of you have gone through enough individually that you can get through this together; you just have to be there for each other. It'll be okay."

After explaining everything to his most trusted friend, Shamar felt relieved that he had finally been able to get it all out of his system. He had always been an emotional person, having been raised by his mother. It was the Gangster Disciples and other neighborhood OGs who taught him everything he knew about being a man. In the streets, he couldn't afford to show feelings. As Kaduwey would say, "Feelings will get you killed."

"All right, folk, enough talking about feelings. You cried it out; now, let's get back to this money. You blowing my high," Kaduwey said, laughing. "You gonna be straight my nig, all right?" he added, trying to redirect the conversation.

Shamar agreed. It was time to check out the whips he had for him to pick from so he could run the errands he had planned for that evening.

They walked to the garage in the back of the trap house where there were two cars hidden under dusty cloths.

"Aw, yeah, what you hiding under there, Wey? Let me find out you still got it."

Kaduwey smiled, looking almost as excited as Shamar appeared to be. He knew what the "it" was Shamar was referring to. Under the first cloth sat an '87 box Chevy Caprice with a candy-apple red custom paint job and matching rims.

Shamar's eyes lit up, and memories resurfaced in his mind, taking him back to the first pack he'd ever moved. He was staring at the first car he had ever bought with his own money. Kaduwey knew how much it meant to Shamar, so he restored it and kept it for him. "Man, bruh, this is crazy! Thanks, yo," Shamar exclaimed, giving Kaduwey some dap and a hug, thanking him for looking out for him. For the moment, everything was back to normal for them; it was like the old days. While they celebrated, an all-too-familiar feeling came over Shamar. It made the hairs on the back of his neck stand up. He began to scan the area for something out of the ordinary.

"Yo, G, what's up? What's wrong? You got that look in your eyes," Kaduwey inquired.

"I don't know, Wey. Something don't feel right. You recognize the blue Impala over there by the train tracks? It's just sitting there and you know a minute too long could mean jump-out boys or a drive-by." If there was one thing the streets and combat taught Shamar, it was to always follow his instincts.

"Naw, man, I don't think so. It is kinda weird them fools just decided to stop right there."

Suddenly, the Impala's tires screeched as the car took off, heading in their direction, swerving left and right and making the right-hand turn just in front of Kaduwey's house. The front and rear driver's side windows rolled down. Just like a scene from a movie, everything seemed to slow down. As the shots rang out, it sounded like a war zone. Bullets ricocheted off of the house and cars as Shamar and Kaduwey ran from the front of the house and ducked behind his SUV parked in the driveway. "I can't believe I let a fool catch me slippin'," Kaduwey shouted, trying to reach for his pistol, which was tucked beside his driver's seat.

Bullets continued to blaze past their heads for what seemed like forever. The smell of gun powder filled the air. Glass shattered all around them as neither were able to return fire. All they could do was stay down and take cover.

The Impala drove completely past the house and headed away from the scene, turning the nearest corner and almost taking out a light pole.

Shamar could see images of Iraq flashing in his mind. This was the reason he left the city in the first place. Kaduwey could be heard breathing heavy and coughing. He moaned and groaned, holding his stomach. When the shooting stopped, everything went quiet. That was, until the sound of sirens could be heard coming from every direction.

"Ahh, I can't believe this! Wey, you good?" Shamar called out from the other side of the SUV as he continued to survey the block, making sure those would-be assassins didn't circle back. He couldn't see Kaduwey on the other side of the vehicle. When he looked over, blood was pouring from his side, and he wasn't moving. He bear crawled around the back of the vehicle and discovered his best friend slumped over on the ground. His breathing was shallow, and suddenly his medic training kicked in as he snatched off his T-shirt, balling it up and pressing it on top of Kaduwey's wound.

Shamar got on his phone and called 911, giving them the details. The police and ambulance arrived while he was still on the line. The police wouldn't let him ride in the ambulance; but, the last he knew, Kaduwey was still breathing. Shamar called and told Jelisa to meet him as he rushed over to the ER.

The waiting room was full of police and all of the homies from the block. Jelisa tried consoling Kaduwey's girlfriend, Ashley. As they sat in the waiting area, Shamar fortified himself in a corner. Jelisa cautiously approached and sat down next to him.

"Baby, you okay?" she said, placing her hand on his knee. "I'm so sorry about your friend. Is there anything I can do?"

Shamar was growing more irritated by the second. He kept his head down and whispered under his breath, "What you could do is get your hand off of me."

Jelisa was offended. She leaned back, scrunching her nose up. Shamar checked himself. "My bad, baby girl. I didn't mean to take it out on you. I'm just saying, I've been home two days and look at everything that's happened. I flipped out on you, Wey's lying up in there with holes in him, and I'm supposed to be here trying to keep things together. Why is this happening to me?" Shamar lamented.

"Baby, I wish I could make it better, but I know I can't. Don't worry about what happened with us earlier. I know you would never hurt me on purpose. I just think you need to take some time to really get away from all of this. Let's pray your friend pulls through, and then we can pick somewhere and just go. Okay?" Jelisa did her best to comfort her brokenhearted soldier, but the best she could do was just be there for him. Shamar was slowly shrinking away into his own shadow, reaching the darkest places of his mind.

A nurse came out a few hours later to deliver an update to Kaduwey's family. He must have had angels around him because she said he should make a full recovery, but it would be touch and go for the time being. Everyone looked at Shamar for some kind of confirmation as to how to react. He stood with his arms folded and a blank stare on his face, still visibly disturbed. The family sat and stood around crying and hugging each other in disbelief. They finally let the family go back and see Kaduwey. Shamar stayed behind out of respect for them.

Kaduwey asked for Shamar to come into his room after he'd had a chance to talk with his family. "What's good, folk? Why you standing way over there? Do I look that bad?" Kaduwey said jokingly as Shamar remained in the doorway.

His mind was telling his feet to walk, but seeing his brother laid up with tubes everywhere paralyzed him. "I'm cool, bruh," he said, inching his way closer to his partner. The only thing he could think of was the beeping sound of the machine next to the bed. "Wey, you sure you good? I don't want to touch nothing or mess nothing up." Shamar nervously walked to his bedside and sat down in the chair next to him. You would think with being a medic he'd be used to seeing things like this. However, this wasn't like any situation he'd been in before. It was his best friend, not some random civilian on the battlefield. It was his brother, and he never imagined he would ever see him like this. Kaduwey's mother and girlfriend stood off to the side as the friends talked.

"I can't believe this happened, man. I should have been strapped. I should have done something," Shamar repented. He was feeling guilty for not being able to protect his friend; much like he felt when he found out Omar had been killed. He wished he could have been there as well.

Kaduwey appreciated his concern, but he wasn't much for the dramatics stuff. "Look, G, I know you're feeling some type of way about all of this. But trust me; it's already taken care of, ya dig? But I need you to do something for me."

Shamar glanced over with a puzzled look on his face.

"I know you don't like talking about it, but I'm telling you that you need to handle that Chrissy situation."

"Wey, come on now, man, I told you—"

Struggling to sit up, Kaduwey cut him off. "I know, I know, but hear me out. Man, lying up here with the holes and tubes in me gave me a lot to think about." He let out a gut-wrenching cough, sounding like he was about to spit up one of his lungs. "You need to find out the truth about that little girl. You can't let her get away with avoiding you and the truth. You keep on worrying about messing her family up, but it's going to tear your family apart in the end."

Shamar remained silent, replaying memories of the last encounter with Chrissy. "All right, man. You ain't going to let this go, are you? This better not blow up in my face. I know that much."

"It won't. Trust me." He let out another violent cough, this time spitting up blood all over himself.

"Wey, you all right, man? Nurse!" Shamar shouted.

The coughing continued, becoming more painful; and the machines in the room beeped faster. When the nurse arrived, she asked everyone to leave the room. Kaduwey's mother and girlfriend were stricken with fear as they were ushered out of the room. Shamar's heart dropped to the bottom of his stomach as he followed them. He paced back and forth, trying not to add to the family's worry. Panic filled the waiting area as the curtains were drawn while the medical staff continued to work.

Twenty minutes later, a doctor emerged from the room with a disappointed look on his face. "I'm sorry, everyone. There has been a change in Mr. Jones's condition. There was some internal bleeding, which we've managed to stop, and he is still breathing on his own. But, unfortunately, he isn't responding."

While the doctor was still talking, Shamar got up, stormed out of the waiting area, and left the building. Jelisa, who was around the corner in another hall on the phone with Shawnie, ran behind him, following him to his car. All Shamar heard was "coma" and "we'll have to wait." Everything else was a blur.

Jelisa finally caught up with him. "Baby, wait up! Hold up, honey. It's going to be okay, baby," she said, rubbing small circles on the middle of his back.

Shamar ignored her attempt to encourage him. He climbed into his car, followed by her climbing into the passenger's seat, and they drove home in silence. Jelisa knew better than to press the issue, so she left Shamar to his thoughts. He slept through the night with only one other thing on his mind: Chrissy.

It didn't take long for the hood to find out who was responsible for the attempted assassination. One of Kaduwey's many enemies from Gary had put some of his goons on him. By the end of the night, the two men responsible were floating somewhere off the coast of Lake Michigan. Street justice came swiftly when it came to someone as respected as Kaduwey.

The next morning, Shamar awoke with a massive headache and a knot in the pit of his stomach. With Jelisa gone to the shop for the rest of the day, he was faced with his friend's last words to him. He questioned if he was really prepared to relive the madness that had once ensued between him and Chrissy. She, being the live wire she was, came fully packaged with years of self-hate and low self-esteem. She hated her black heritage that made her who she was, and she looked at every black man with disdain because of it which was odd to Shamar because she always had a thing for him.

Shamar logged on to his laptop and pulled up his Facebook account, which he rarely used. He knew to be careful contacting Chrissy as she was known for blocking people and later stalking their page to make sure she wasn't being blasted over the Web.

After some brief research, a picture of Chrissy Reynolds came up as her profile picture. Shamar sighed as he anticipated her reaction to him reaching out. She was married, so it would make sense for her to be defensive of the life she had built over the years. Selecting her page, he clicked on message and hesitated before typing.

Hey, Chrissy? he typed, and then anxiously awaited her response.

What? she replied.

What you mean what? We need to talk ASAP. Shamar couldn't stand when females were short with him, but he was careful not to push her too soon.

Shamar, what do you want?

He wasn't in the mood to argue with her, but he knew she was going to test him and he was determined not to fall for it. His face frowned up as he changed his posture, preparing to dig into her.

Chrissy, stop playing with me, hear? We need to talk about shorty and don't blow me off 'cause I'm not backing off of this. Call me now. You got the number. You've got five minutes. Try me if you want to.

Chrissy didn't respond right away, and Shamar wondered if he had blown it. The moments that passed were hell to live through. After ten minutes, his cell phone vibrated.

"Hello? Chrissy, what's good?"

"Shamar, stop talking like we cool or something!" Chrissy snapped. "The only reason I called you is because you putting me in a bad situation. You know this ain't even fair. I told you she ain't yours."

Shamar figured she would plead with him to change his mind, but it was already settled. He owed it to himself to find out. Plus, the weight of Kaduwey's words wouldn't let him leave it alone. "Chrissy, I'm not trying to argue with you; and stop trying to put this all on me. You're acting like I'm doing something wrong to you. We in this together whether you like it or not. At the end of the day, you have to prove me wrong."

Chrissy was starting to get agitated by Shamar's nonchalant attitude. "Shamar, how many times do I have to tell you that she don't look like you? That child is white, period, point blank. So I don't have to prove nothing to you. Now, why don't you just leave me and my family alone?" Her voice began to tremble the more she tried to convince him to let it go.

"Chrissy, you already know what's next if you keep testing me. You know me. I don't play about my kids."

Chrissy began to panic. She knew exactly what he would do next, and she couldn't afford to have her secret blasted all over the city. If Shamar took her to court, there was a strong chance he could be right, and she'd have to own up to everything. "Shamar, please don't ruin my life or my daughter's life. I swear to God she is not yours. If she were darker, maybe I could see that; but she don't even look like she has any black in her. And, no offense, but I'm so glad she doesn't. I would just kill myself if I even thought there was a possibility she was yours. I'm sorry you feel this way. But I promise you she's not yours. Just let it go," Chrissy pleaded with him with everything she had in her, but he wouldn't budge. "Shamar, let it go. Let me go. You don't have to do this. Just leave us alone! Don't call me, don't message me, just leave me alone. She's not yours!" Chrissy proclaimed, hanging up on him.

Frustrated, Shamar slammed his fist on the computer desk and let out a loud grunt. "This girl is going to make me hurt her. I guess it's business as usual. Let's make it happen," he said, giving himself a pep talk.

He looked across the room at Mya, who had fallen asleep playing in the middle of the living room. As he approached her, he stood there staring at her, trying to see if there was any resemblance to Chrissy's daughter. The uncertainty was driving him crazy. But, for now, there was nothing he could do. He'd have to handle things once he was back from Iraq for good.

Chapter Twelve

By the end of the first week, Shamar was beyond ready to leave Indiana. Who would've thought he'd actually be looking forward to returning to Iraq with his unit? Things between him and Jelisa were strained, and he knew at some point his conscience would force him to tell her about Chrissy and her daughter. They hadn't talked about the fact that another guy answered her phone. With everything that was going on it was the last thing on his mind. Compared to everything else it was minute.

While he was on the way to meet with up with Jelisa's father, he stopped by the shop to pay her a surprise visit. Making his way through the parking lot, Shamar caught a glimpse of Jelisa through the front window. She looked so unhappy standing behind her client and looking up every so often. As he caught the door behind someone coming out, Shamar managed to get near Jelisa's workstation undetected.

The women looking on watched with envy as Shamar crept up behind her, holding a bouquet of pink roses. He admired her curvy hips and the way her smock hugged her chest. Jelisa had no idea her lover was standing there, ready to romance her; but as a shop door swung closed, a cold breeze let her catch a whiff of Shamar's cologne. It stopped her in her tracks as the aroma gave her chills.

"Um, well, look at that. What I gotta do to get with that?" Shamar said, disguising his voice.

Not taking too kindly to the offensive gesture, Jelisa, barely looking over her shoulder, responded with an attitude, "I know you're not talking to me like that."

Trying to push her to pop off, Shamar slapped her right butt cheek.

Jelisa immediately spun around, fully prepared to snap. Before she could get another word out, Shamar grabbed her by the waist, bringing her closer to him. He planted a romantic kiss on her lips, and it was as if her body completely melted.

"Oh my God. Shamar, what are you doing? Boy, you better quit playing with me. I thought I was tripping at first when I smelled your cologne. What are you doing here?" Jelisa displayed a huge smile and was filled with excitement, seeing him standing there.

"I just wanted to come and see about you. I want to take you out to lunch so we can talk. You up for it?"

"Yeah, we can do that. Give me like fifteen minutes and I'll be ready. Where is Mya, with my mom?"

Just then, Donny appeared from the back room, talking on his cell phone. Before Shamar could answer Jelisa's question about Mya, his attention was drawn to Donny, who was now standing across the room, laughing. Shamar's grin turned into a frown as he recognized that voice.

"Baby, what's wrong with you? Why you looking like that?" Jelisa asked as a look of worry covered her face. She knew that look, and it meant things were about to go from good to horrible real soon.

Shamar dropped the flowers, pushed away from Jelisa and, without breaking stride, he engaged Donny. Donny, still on the phone, was caught off guard and had no idea why he was being approached.

"Say, homeboy, so you like to play on phones, huh?"

It took a second for it to register with Donny that Shamar was talking to him. Before he could react, Shamar rushed him, landing a furious three piece to his mouth. The shop erupted in panic and confusion. The women screamed, and the other barbers struggled to pull him off of Donny.

Jelisa was frantic, yelling at him to let him go. When they were finally able to separate the two, Donny lay bloodied and bruised on the floor in a fetal position. Shamar pushed his way through the crowd, storming out the door. Jelisa followed him. He marched down the street breathing heavy, his hands throbbing.

"Shamar, will you stop? What the hell is wrong with you? You can't just go beating people up like that. Are you crazy?"

Shamar stopped in his tracks and snatched Jelisa by her coat. "You're right I'm crazy. Crazy for thinking I could leave you here by yourself and not have to worry about you creeping."

"Shamar, what are you talking about? Ain't nobody creeping. Where is all of this coming from?"

"Jelisa, you know what I'm talking about. The last time I tried to call you before I came home, that clown answered your phone. Now go ahead and try to lie your way out of this one."

Jelisa's heart sank to the bottom of her stomach. She knew she shouldn't have believed

Donny when he said he didn't have her phone that night she couldn't find it. "Baby, please let me explain. It's not what you think. I . . . I went to a party he had at his house and—"

"You was at his house, too? Jelisa, I swear you hella goofy. What were you thinking?" Shamar was heated.

Jelisa knew that if she didn't calm him down, it was only going to get worse. "Baby, I swear to you I didn't do nothing with him. He invited everyone from the shop to his party. I told you I was going, anyway. Practically the whole neighborhood was there. Baby, you've got to believe me," she pleaded with him. With a look of desperation in her eyes, she looked into his soul.

He didn't know if she really was innocent, as she claimed; but when he thought about the fact that he would eventually have to tell her about Chrissy, he didn't want this to be thrown back in his face. "Look, Jelisa, I'm not really feeling like dealing with this right now. I trust you, but I don't like that dude. I never have. If you tell me nothing happened, then I don't have any choice but to believe you. But I'm telling you, Jelisa, you better check him before I hurt him."

"All right, Shamar. God," she said under her breath.

Shamar walked back to his car, got in, and sped off. Jelisa went back into the shop to try to smooth things over with Donny. How mad could he really be since he'd lied about having her phone anyway? When she got to her workstation, Donny was in front of his mirror attempting to clean himself up. He looked her way, embarrassed and ashamed that he had just gotten the beats put on him.

"So what do you have to say now, Donny? I see the look on your face; don't even try to blame this on me," she told him with a smirk.

"Jelisa, don't play with me. Homeboy lucky I didn't up the burner on him. Go on somewhere with that." Donny's pride was hurt; but no matter how slick he was talking to Jelisa, he and everybody present knew he wouldn't back up anything he was saying. Donny was just a loudmouth pretty boy, and Shamar's and Kaduwey's names still carried weight in the city. For him, this meant he'd just have to eat this one and charge it to the game. He knew Shamar had just given him a pass; the best he could do was leave well enough alone.

"You shouldn't have lied about my phone. Now I've got to deal with my man thinking I'm creeping with you. Thanks a lot!"

She did her best to forget about the drama that had just popped off as she finished up her last few clients and headed to her mother's to pick Mya up. She hoped Shamar would calm down and they would be able to put the day's events behind them. Donny messing with her phone was the last thing she needed between her and Shamar. All that was going on with Shamar and Kaduwey, the issues with Sandra, and the fact that Shamar was getting ready to have to go back to Iraq, it all was becoming too much for her.

It had been months since Shamar had spoken to Pete; and, after the blowup at the shop, he needed a guy to talk to. It was poor timing, but after driving around for hours he found himself parked in front of Pete's house. Pete sat on the porch, as usual, smoking his pipe. When Shamar saw him sitting there, he began to rehearse what he would say when they spoke. *Man, I don't know if I should even talk to him about this. He already don't like me.* Shamar got out and made his way up the sidewalk, walking with his head down and a slow bop.

"What's up, soldier boy, how's it going? What brings you around these parts? There must be something wrong."

"Hey, Mr. Adams, how you doing, sir?" Shamar didn't look too enthused as he walked up onto the porch. "I was wondering if I could rap with you for a minute."

"Yeah, sure, son. Have a seat." Pete motioned for Shamar to take a seat in the chair next to him. He took a puff from his pipe and said, "So what's going on in your world? I know you and I don't have too much to say to each other, so it must have to do with my daughter. So what's going on?"

Shamar hesitated for a minute before answering. "Well, sir, it's Jelisa. I mean, I don't know what's going on with her. She keeps popping off at me. I've only been back a week, and something just doesn't feel right. I just had to go at some dude's head because she done messed around and got dude playing on her phone while I was gone. I can't take it. I just don't know what to do with her. Know what I'm saying?"

Pete looked over at Shamar nonchalantly and grinned. "Son, don't worry about that. I know my daughter and one thing she isn't is a liar. If she says nothing's going on, then that's it. You know, Shamar, you and I haven't had too many real conversations so I know this must really be bothering you. You have to see things from her perspective and know that she isn't used to the military or the married life. I never said anything about the two of you getting married because I knew your dad and your uncles, so I knew you came from good peoples. But I knew there would be some challenges for y'all being that you both are so young."

Shamar hung his head, contemplating all that was being said. He knew in the beginning that it was risky to marry so young, let alone move Jelisa away from her family. However, Shamar had already seen his share of marriages fail due to deployments, and he couldn't stand the thought of it happening to him. "Mr. Adams, I know Jelisa's a good girl and, just like her mom and sisters, she's got a mouth on her. You know how it is. I just want to make sure her and baby girl are straight. As for that clown she works with, I don't trust him, and I really don't want her around him at all. I don't think I can do the rest of my time over there worrying about what she might be doing. She's still human, and I don't expect her to stay cooped up in the house the whole time I'm gone, either. What do you think I should do?" Shamar looked up at Pete, and the look of concern on his face showed that it was really getting to him.

"Look, Shamar, I can't tell you what to do about your own marriage; that's not my place.

My marriage to Sandra was ruined, in part, because we allowed other people to get involved with things we should have handled ourselves. You have to take her and sit down with her. You two have to be honest with each other about everything because if you don't, you will have to face it eventually. I promise you this: if you don't deal with the issues now, they will only get worse, especially with you being separated."

When Shamar considered what Pete was saying, he thought about the fallout he would have to face if Jelisa found out about Chrissy and her daughter. With her being the live wire she was, it would only turn out bad if she didn't hear it from him. The only problem was he would first have to prove that the little girl was his. He ran the risk of messing up two homes whether he was right or wrong. If he was wrong, Chrissy's so-called marriage would be destroyed, and her relationship with her daughter wouldn't be the same. If he was right, the same things could possibly happen. Either way, it could go bad.

"Yeah, you right, sir. I just don't want to leave next week with all of this friction between us. If she isn't up to anything, I don't want to give her a reason to do something crazy. I need to go see her and straighten things out. We've come too far to let something like this mess it up."

Shamar stood up, and Pete followed suit. Shamar stuck his hand out, reaching for a handshake, and said, "Well, sir, I appreciate you talking with me. I know we don't usually vibe like that, but I'll make sure I take care of this before I leave."

Pete reciprocated and met his handshake and replied, "Anytime, son. You just make sure you take care of my daughter and my grandbaby. I know you will make the right decision. You take care of yourself, you hear?"

Shamar nodded as he turned to walk to his car. He knew better than to share with Pete about the recent event between him and Jelisa. He would've tried to kill him for putting his hands on her. Besides that, even though he promised Jelisa he'd talk to Pete, his pride would not let him bring up the nightmares. Leaving well enough alone, he waved good-bye to Pete as he drove off, headed back to Jelisa's apartment.

Jelisa arrived at Sandra's house just as it was starting to get dark. She had not heard from Shamar for the rest of the day and was beginning to worry about whether he really believed her. When she walked into the living room, Sandra and Shawnie were watching TV while Mya played with her dolls. It seemed like everything was normal, but normal didn't feel right. Something was off; she just couldn't tell what it was.

"Hey, y'all, what's up?" she said, sitting down next to Shawnie. Mya dropped her toys and ran over to her with a smile, climbing onto her lap.

"Hey, girl, what's up?" Shawnie said, barely taking her eyes away from the TV.

"Hey, Mama, how you doing?"

Sandra sat across from them in the corner, smoking a cigarette. She looked over at Jelisa, giving her a simple, "Hey, Jelisa." Sandra still hadn't gotten over their blowup and was only being civil with her because of Mya, at the request of Shawnie.

"Shawnie, girl, tell me why Shamar popped up at the shop today."

Shawnie's attention quickly left the show; automatically, she knew something was wrong. Sandra cut her eyes toward them, trying to listen in.

"Aw, hell, what happened?"

"Girl, remember I told you I thought I left my phone at the shop one night awhile back?"

Shawnie nodded.

"Well, I had a feeling Donny had taken it home with him 'cause I tracked it with my GPS and his address came up. But, of course, he denied having it when I asked him about it. So anyway, apparently Shamar tried to call me that night. So when he came to the shop, Donny was on the phone, and I guess Shamar recognized his voice. Girl, he beat the spit out of his mouth right there in the shop." Her attempt at whispering failed as Mya's ears perked up when she heard Shamar's name.

Realizing that Mya was listening, Jelisa said, "My-My, go upstairs with TT."

She fumbled around with her dolls for a few seconds before making her way upstairs.

"Jelisa, are you serious? Please tell me you not messing with this fool."

"Shawnie, come on now; what you take me for? I ain't stupid. You know this city is too small to be trying to creep with somebody. Shamar would kill me if he found out I was cheating on him. Matter of fact, that's what he asked me. Trust me, Donny is not worth the headache."

Sandra scoffed, mumbling something under her breath. Jelisa looked over at her and quickly dismissed her.

Shawnie shook her head in disbelief. "Jelisa, I told you to stop playing with that boy. He has enough to worry about being overseas. Now you got him thinking you messing around. Are you trying to make this man hurt you?"

"Shawnie, I'm serious, I am not messing with this dude. I just hope Shamar believes me. He's only got a few more days until he has to go back and I am not trying to have him leave with this hanging between us," Jelisa said, lowering her head.

"What's wrong?" Shawnie asked.

"I'm still thinking about Reggie popping up at my place. I can't shake it. I hope he ain't up to nothing; but, knowing him, he probably is. I just hope Shamar is gone by the time he tries something."

Shawnie looked over at her, puzzled. "Shamar doesn't know?" she asked.

Jelisa didn't answer; her head remained down.

"Jelisa, come on. Look, I'm not trying to get in your business, but you're digging yourself a deep hole right now. I just hope this stuff doesn't blow up in your face."

After thinking for a second, Jelisa raised her head and worry was painted all over her face. She knew there was a chance that this could all blow up, but she was betting on Shamar being gone before she'd have to confront her demons. If it all worked out according to her plan, it would all be dealt with, and they would be on their way back to Fort Riley. Shamar wouldn't have to know anything. It would all be behind her.

"I know, Shawnie. I just need to hold off until after he leaves. I'll handle everything else. Just please don't say nothing to him."

"Girl, you know I ain't going to say nothing; it ain't my business. But you better do something 'cause you know people around here can't hold water."

"Yeah, this is stressing me out. I need a drink. Mama, what you got to drink in there?"

Sandra looked up at her and shrugged her shoulders, saying, "Girl, stop acting like you're a visitor or something. Go on in there and see." She looked like she wanted to say something else but she held her peace. Both Shawnie and Jelisa picked up on it, but neither spoke up. Better to keep the peace than force the issue.

After driving around for a couple of hours, Shamar found himself driving down Michigan Boulevard in a daze. With just a few days before he would have to return to Iraq, he was faced with the decision of whether to tell Jelisa about Chrissy and the possibility of her daughter being his. If Jelisa wasn't already cheating, the shock alone could be enough to push her to do it, especially with him being gone until next fall.

Shamar pulled over in front of what used to be the Harborside projects but was now an open park owned by the local casino. He found a bench and posted up, watching the cars speed by.

Man, now what am I going to do? I don't want to go through all of this with Chrissy and then find out shorty ain't mine. But, then again, I'm not trying to give her a pass either 'cause I'm gonna be pissed as if I find out later that she is. This is so stupid.

Shamar continued conversing with himself, in his mind, trying to decide what to do. By midnight, he had made his mind up to pay Chrissy a visit and get the answer to the question that could make or break his marriage. He had no idea how it would play out, but he had no other choice; it had to be done.

Content with his decision, Shamar made his way back to Jelisa's place. He arrived to a cold, empty apartment. Jelisa and Mya were nowhere to be found. She drank herself to sleep at Sandra's house, worried about what Shamar must have been thinking. Shamar, hoping the next day would be better, fell asleep on the couch in the living room.

The next morning, Shamar was startled out of his sleep by his phone vibrating. "Hello?" he said, clearing his throat and sitting up, resting his elbows on his knees. "What's up, Ashley? How you doing? What's the news?" He knew something was up for her to be calling him.

"He's awake, and he wants to see you. Hurry, we don't have much time," Ashley said. She spoke with no emotion, only a sense of urgency. Her voice suggested that she had accepted the fact that this would be their final conversation.

Shamar's head dropped, and tears poured from his eyes as he processed the news. He rushed over to the hospital, blowing through every stop sign and light. When he made it to Kaduwey's room, he asked everyone to leave. The damage from the bullet wounds was worse than everyone thought, and his body couldn't recover from the surgery. He didn't look like himself and Shamar struggled to keep eye contact as he fought back the tears.

"What's good, folk?" Kaduwey whispered; his voice was raspy and hoarse. "Yo, bruh, it ain't looking good for me. Guess I should've cut back on the herb and double cupping. That lean messed my system up. I don't know how much longer I got."

"Wey, don't talk like that, man. You gonna be all right, dawg, just hold on."

"Look, man, I don't know what the big Man Upstairs has for me, but I need you to do something for me."

Shamar stepped closer to his bed and sat down next to him. "What's up, man? If it's about Chrissy, I already got that covered. I'm gonna deal with that today. I just need you to pull through." Kaduwey didn't respond, and Shamar continued. "I know what I have to do; I just have to make sure I go about it the right way, you know what I'm saying? Wey! Wey!" Shamar began to panic. Kaduwey wasn't responding; he stared up at the ceiling, not even moving.

"Hey, somebody, help!" Shamar called out. "Come on, man, don't do this to me. Wake up, man!" Shamar shook him, trying to wake him, but nothing worked. He had slipped back into a coma. What was he trying to ask him to do?

As the nurses tended to him, standing by helpless became too much for Shamar. He quickly departed the hospital. Once he reached his car, he searched through his phone to find Chrissy's number. He was now even more motivated to get to the bottom of their situation. Shamar knew that calling her to let her know he was on the way to see her would spook her and she would make sure he missed her. He knew she worked for a manufacturing company; and, after a little research, it wasn't too hard to find out where she lived.

It was just before two o'clock when Shamar pulled into the parking lot of a local bread-making company. As he sat in the parking lot next to the modest factory building, his mind raced as he anticipated the outcome of this encounter. *Lord, please don't let this girl act up out here. I ain't trying to go to jail.*

Shortly after two o'clock, people began to emerge from the building. He didn't know what Chrissy was driving so he got out and leaned back on the hood of his car. He spotted her coming across the lot, laughing it up with one of her coworkers. She looked as if she didn't have a care in the world. Seeing that burned Shamar; the nerve of her prancing around like she had everything together. She knew what she had done by refusing to discuss their possible child with him. It was as if she didn't feel like she had any explaining to do. His face frowned slightly as she proceeded across the lot.

Chrissy's face went blank as their eyes met and her heart dropped to the pit of her stomach. Her first thought was to ignore him, but she knew he wouldn't stand for that. She lowered her head and slowed her pace down to a halt. "What are you doing here, Shamar? I thought I told you to leave me alone. We don't have anything to talk about. Are you serious?" she protested, pouting with her hand on her hip.

Shamar pushed himself off of the hood, stuffing his keys in his pocket. He stepped closer until he was only inches away, towering over her. "Chrissy, do I look serious? Stop playing with me. Now, we need to talk, and we can handle this between the two of us, or it can get as messy as you want it to. I'm trying to be nice about the situation because your dude had nothing to do with this."

Chrissy was puzzled. "What are you talking about? Don't bring my man into this. That's why I keep telling you to let it go. He doesn't know anything about us, and it needs to stay that way. Why are you trying to ruin my life?" Chrissy began to get loud, attracting stares from her coworkers.

"Chrissy, lower your voice. Don't forget who the hell you're talking to right now. I'm not in the mood to be playing around with you. You can pop off all you want in those messages because I can't reach you. I wish you would try that mess with me now. Whether you like it or not, we're going to deal with this. Now, are you going to give me a DNA test or do I need to get that paperwork started?"

Shamar had determination written all over his face, and Chrissy knew he wasn't going to let up. She had pleaded with him to leave it alone. If it came out that she had a kid with Shamar, the whole city would soon know, and her reputation would be ruined. She made one final attempt at changing his mind.

"Look, Shamar, I know how you are about your family and I'm sorry you feel like there's a possibility; but, I swear on everything I love, my daughter is not yours. She doesn't even look like you or your daughter. Hell, she don't even look like she has a black father. Frankly, I'm glad she doesn't, which is why I'm begging you not to do this to me. You're going to ruin my life over nothing. Leave it alone, Shamar; just leave it alone, please." Chrissy's eyes welled up as she backed away from him, heading toward her car.

Seeing the look on her face made him start having second thoughts. He watched helplessly as she walked away, not knowing what he should do next. *Man, she really ain't budging. What if I am wrong? I mean, there is a good chance I could be. I don't want to be the reason her family is torn apart.* The more he thought about it, the more doubt invaded his conscience.

Things had just gotten more complicated; and, from this point on, he had to play it safe. He got back in his car and drove back over to Jelisa's apartment, stopping by Jo Jo's to grab something to eat.

Chapter Thirteen

Jelisa and Mya made it home around noon. There was an awkwardly parked black Cadillac in front of her apartment. She knew pretty much every one of her neighbors and their vehicles, but this one was not familiar. She held Mya close to her, surveying her surroundings as she made her way up to her door. Cautiously going inside, Jelisa could feel something was wrong; there was a strange scent in the air. It was strange but familiar, and her heart began to beat rapidly.

"My-My, come here. Come sit down on the couch for Mommy. Don't move."

Jelisa maneuvered through the apartment, investigating every corner of every room. When she had completed the search of her room, she went to her dresser drawer to retrieve the .38 she kept for self-defense. Although she hadn't found anything, something still didn't feel right. Jelisa made her way back toward the front, and there was an eerie silence. It was quiet, a little too quiet.

"Mya! What are you doing, baby? My . . ." Jelisa was suddenly overcome with panic and rage. *Oh my God, no!* she screamed inside. "What are you doing in my house, Reggie? You've got a lot of nerve. Put my daughter down right now before I blow your head off!" Jelisa was terrified and pissed, and Mya sitting in his lap was the only thing stopping her from blowing his head off.

Reggie chuckled with a sinister grin. "Now, now, we don't want to take it there, do we? She is so precious; she looks just like you." Reggie stroked Mya's long, curly hair, never taking his eyes off of Jelisa. She cringed, and her heart sank deeper with every stroke of his hand. "Now why don't you take your finger off that trigger before you piss me off and things get really messy in here?" Reggie stated firmly.

Jelisa submitted, tucking the pistol in her back pocket. She took a deep breath and asked, "What do you want, Reggie?"

"I just came by to check on my baby girl. You know I've waited a long time to see you, and you're just as beautiful as I remembered. How is your mother doing, still hanging tough with Jack Daniels?" Jelisa was beginning to grow restless, and it was all over her face. Picking up on her impatience, Reggie cut through all of the small talk. "Look, angel, I know you haven't told your brave little soldier boy about your little secret, have you?"

Jelisa dropped her head. She couldn't believe she was standing in the presence of the man who had robbed her of her innocence. Having to face him was torture, but it was past time for this little reunion to be over.

"What do you want from me, Reggie? I'm over this right now. You need to put my daughter down and get the hell out of my house."

Reggie stood up with a grin on his face. Still holding Mya in his arms, he walked toward Jelisa, backing her into a wall. As he invaded her personal space, her heart beat faster. She could barely breathe as he caressed her cheek. "You know exactly what I want, and if you don't want your precious little toy soldier to find out about your secret—"

Jelisa took this opportunity to snatch Mya out of his arms. She put the pistol to Reggie's chest. "Get out! Reggie, I swear to God if you come near me or my family again I will kill you! If we cross paths again, the only thing you're going to get from me is a bullet." Jelisa's parental instincts were in full force; and, as terrified as she was, she was willing to die to protect the people she loved.

Reggie seemed unfazed. He nodded and grinned, backing away. "All right, angel, I'll be seeing you. You stay pretty, you hear me? Don't hurt nobody now."

When Reggie closed the door behind him, Jelisa took another deep breath. As she exhaled, she held Mya as tight as she could. She tucked the pistol back into her pocket, slid down the wall, and sat on the floor crying. She wished at that moment that Shamar had been there to protect her. As devoted as he was to the Army and Kaduwey, she never seemed to be as important to him. She was growing tired of being left alone when she needed to feel safe, and this was the last straw.

She sat there for the next fifteen minutes trying to regain her composure. Suddenly, she heard a tugging at the door. The knob turned left and right repeatedly. Panic set in and the thought that Reggie might have come back to finish what he started struck fear in her heart. She reasoned within herself whether she was actually willing to follow through with her previous threats.

Jelisa jumped up and ran into Mya's room. She sat her on her bed and told her to stay put. Locking the door behind her, Jelisa returned to the living room and stood off to the side of the door, hoping to catch the intruder by surprise.

Her heart raced as the visitor struggled to get the door to open. When the door finally opened, Jelisa panicked, and her finger pulled the trigger.

Pow!

Shamar was grazed on the shoulder. He fell over, rolling onto the couch. "What the hell? Ah! Jelisa, what is wrong with you?"

"Oh, my God, Shamar! I'm so sorry. I didn't mean to—"

"What you mean you didn't mean to?" Shamar said, recovering and standing to his feet. He snatched the gun away from her, grabbing her by the throat and forcing her back to the wall. Slamming the door shut behind him, he looked at her with rage in his eyes. "Jelisa, have you lost your mind? First of all, what are you doing with this?" he questioned, displaying the pistol. "Secondly, what happened to you to make you feel like you needed to use it now?"

Jelisa hesitated as she tried to quickly come up with a lie. "Baby, I swear nothing happened. I was just trying to load it. When you came in the door, you surprised me, and it just went off. I swear, Shamar, that's what happened. My dad gave me this gun."

Seeing that the bullet had barely grazed him, Shamar shook it off. "Go get me a bandage. I can't believe you, girl. You are not allowed to play with guns no more. Matter of fact, where is Mya before you mess around and hurt somebody?"

"She's in her room, playing, baby. I swear I didn't mean it. I'm so sorry. Are you okay?" Jelisa couldn't believe what had just happened. Her adrenaline was still pumping and she felt a sense of both fear and excitement. On one hand, she could have killed Shamar; however, all anxiety concerning pulling the trigger was now gone.

Jelisa walked into the bathroom and grabbed her first aid kit from the medicine cabinet. As she turned and made her way back into the living room, she stopped to listen for Mya playing on the other side of her bedroom door. It was unusually quiet. Being by herself for this amount of time Jelisa would have expected at least a little bit of banging. Suddenly, her eyes got big as she noticed a bullet hole in the center of Mya's bedroom door.

She dropped the first aid kit and slowly reached for the door handle. Her hand shaking rapidly she could hardly force herself to turn it. *No, no, no. God, no, please don't let her be hurt,* she pleaded in her mind.

Jelisa opened the door slowly, revealing her baby lying on the bed, motionless. Her heart sank.

She gasped for air, holding her stomach with one hand and covering her mouth with the other. She began to fear the worst as she stepped closer to the bed.

"Mya, baby, are you okay? Come on, baby, wake up. Wake up for Mommy." Her voice trembled.

"What's taking so long, Jelisa? Come on, man, I'm bleeding all over myself," Shamar shouted. Shamar stood up and walked to the hallway and discovered Jelisa standing next to Mya's bed looking like she'd seen a ghost.

"Baby, what's wrong? What are you doing?" he asked. Just then he noticed the hole in the door. "Jelisa, what happened?" Shamar ran over to the bedroom door. "Oh my God, Mya, baby, no! Please no!"

Shamar froze, fearing the worst. He cautiously approached the bed and touched her seemingly lifeless body as Jelisa stood unable to move. His heart pounded, and his stomach twisted in knots. He placed his hand on her back, using his other hand to turn her over. Jelisa, still in the background, watched in agony, also fearing the worst.

When Shamar turned her over, much to his relief, she was breathing. When he called out to her, she slowly opened her eyes. She smiled, and her face lit up when she realized it was him.

They both breathed a sigh of relief and they were thankful she was okay. Shamar grabbed Mya from the bed, holding her tightly and kissing her repeatedly on her face and cheeks. Jelisa watched as he interacted with his daughter. She nervously reached out to touch her.

"Jelisa, don't you ever do anything like that again. You hear me? I don't know what I would do if something were to happen to one of y'all," he said, pulling her close.

"Yes, baby, I know. It's entirely my fault. I promise it won't happen again," she said, hugging them.

That Wednesday turned out to be one of the most difficult days of Shamar's trip home. In just one day he would have to head to Chicago to prepare to go back to Iraq, and he felt like he hadn't accomplished anything at all. His wife was an emotional wreck, and he couldn't help but feel like she was keeping something from him. He intended to find out exactly what it was. Chrissy was still resisting him, claiming that her daughter wasn't his and giving him no reasonable proof that she wasn't. Kaduwey's life hung in the balance as he struggled to live, and he had no idea how that was going to turn out.

This young soldier had seen more death and destruction in the little time he had been at home than he had seen in the few months he was in Iraq. It pained him to have to leave with things in Michigan City in the condition they were in. There were questions that still needed to be answered; and, the day before he was to fly out, Shamar sat on Ashley's porch while on the phone with his commander, explaining the recent events to him.

"Sir, I understand it's been two weeks but I really need an extension. I can't leave just yet," Shamar pleaded with him.

Captain Miller tried to understand his plight, but there was only so much he could do. "Look, Sergeant, I'm sorry to hear about your friend, but you know the Army's policy. If they aren't immediate family, there is no way I can approve you staying any longer. You need to be on that plane tomorrow, or you're going to force my hand," Captain Miller explained.

Shamar sat there speechless with his head down and the phone barely touching his cheek. Ashley stood in the doorway behind him with the door partially open, listening to the whole conversation. Suddenly, her phone rang. It was her mother on the phone calling from the hospital. "What? Okay. I'll be right there," she said in a panic just as Shamar was hanging up the phone. "Shamar, we have to go now! Something's wrong with my baby. Please get me to the hospital!"

"What you mean something's wrong? Ashley, what happened? Tell me what's going on," he demanded.

"I don't . . . I don't know. Just get me to the hospital now! We have to go now!" she pleaded.

"Okay, okay, come on. Let's go." Shamar didn't know what to think. He just hoped his friend was going to be okay.

As they raced down the boulevard, all he could think about was being there for his friend. He had nobody besides him and Jelisa. He couldn't bear the thought of losing him. Ashley couldn't believe what she was hearing.

When they arrived at the hospital, Kaduwey's whole family filled the waiting area. His mother and Ashley's mother were consoling each other as Shamar and Ashley walked in. By the looks on everyone's faces, Shamar knew the worst had happened, but it didn't register completely.

"No! Mama, please tell me he's all right," Ashley begged her mother.

Shamar collapsed in the middle of the floor, falling to his knees. He began sobbing in disbelief. Jelisa was blowing his phone up trying to reach him. Everyone was devastated. Kaduwey was gone. They were too late, and Shamar was alone again.

When he got home several hours later, Jelisa sat on the couch, her face covered with traces of dried-up tears. She wanted to be with him, but by the time she'd gotten the news, it was too late, and he'd texted her asking her to wait for him at home.

Things with Jelisa were better but still questionable, and he didn't want to take his pain and frustration out on her. He knew she wanted to be there, but it was just too much for him to handle at once. Shamar just wanted to have some time by himself before he faced her.

Before leaving the hospital, he had to break the news to Ashley that he had to leave the next morning or face a court-martial. He would've have risked it if it were for Jelisa and Mya.

Driving from Michigan City to Chicago seemed like the longest trip ever. It was a heartbreaking scene at the airport terminal as Shamar bid his wife and daughter farewell. Mya was visually bothered as she could tell something was about to change. As he held her in his arms, she wouldn't let him put her down. Jelisa didn't bother holding back her tears. It wouldn't be until fall that they would be able to see him again. Jelisa questioned if she would be able to hold it together until he returned.

"You know I love you, right?" Shamar asked, then kissing Jelisa on the forehead.

"Yeah, I know. I love you more. I don't want you to go," she answered.

"Come on, Jelisa. Don't do this, baby. We only have a few more months, and I'll be home for good. Just hold me down. Okay?"

"Yeah, I guess. You better call me as soon as you land. You hear me?" Jelisa said, poking her lip out in protest.

Once they began to call for passengers to begin boarding, Shamar gave his family one last hug and kiss before walking down the hall, heading for the plane.

Shamar boarded his plane, and it took off heading to Kuwait, where he'd have to drive from there back to Iraq. As the plane settled at its cruising altitude, three questions weighed heavy on his heart: What was Jelisa hiding? What was Kaduwey trying to tell him? And why was Chrissy trying so hard to keep him from finding out the truth about her daughter? Helpless but determined, Shamar was prepared to get answers, even if he had to get them from halfway across the world.

***

Jelisa had trouble sleeping the first couple of days after Shamar went back. She missed him terribly, and she was starting to think the Army life wasn't all that it was cracked up to be. It took a few weeks but eventually Jelisa fell back into her normal routine. It became easier for her to sleep and even Donny began to back off some from his usual flirting. She hadn't heard anything from Reggie, and it seemed as if her life was finally in order.

Yet and still she felt like she needed to get away. Jelisa decided she would take a week's vacation from the shop to go to Indianapolis to spend some time with Shawnie. This was much-needed time away, and she had some things to discuss with her that couldn't be talked about at home.

She was booked up for the next couple of months and, after some planning, it was finally set in stone, and the timing couldn't have been more perfect. The spring weather was starting to set in, and flowers sprouted up everywhere. It was the perfect time to get away. After leaving Mya with their mother and sisters, Jelisa and Shawnie headed to Nap.

When they arrived at the hotel, they checked in and unpacked, ready to hit the town. They found a nice bistro to have lunch at not far from where they were staying. After ordering their food and drinks, the sisters sat and took in the scenery. Shawnie could tell something was bothering Jelisa as she sat quietly, staring out of a nearby window.

"Jelisa, what's wrong with you? Why are you so quiet?"

It took a few seconds for it to register to her that Shawnie was talking to her. She snapped out of her daze and looked over at Shawnie. "Oh, my bad, girl. I was daydreaming. What did you say?"

"That's what I'm talking about. What is wrong with you, girl? You've been sitting there staring out the window ever since we got here. I know something is bothering you. What is it?" Shawnie asked, reaching across the table and placing her hand on top of Jelisa's.

Jelisa had a worried look on her face as she searched her mind for the right words. "I don't know if I can do this anymore, Shawnie. This Army wife stuff ain't what I thought it was going to be. He's gone more than he's home, and I don't want to wake up one morning and find out something happened to him. You get what I'm saying?"

Shawnie nodded her head and replied, "Yeah, I know what you're saying, Jelisa. Don't take this the wrong way, but this is what you signed up for. You married a soldier; deployments and time apart come with the territory. I can see that it's getting to you, but that's why you have to make the most of the time you have with him."

"I tried to. But with everything that was going on, we barely had any time together before he had to go back. I just don't know if I'm cut out for this. Now to make things worse, I think Reggie is back in town. I swear I keep seeing a car just like his everywhere I go, and God only knows, if it is him, what he's up to. He already came to my house twice and—"

Shawnie's face turned sour as she interrupted, saying, "I thought you said he only came by that one time before I got there. Why didn't you tell me this, Jelisa?"

"Because I knew you would overreact just like you're about to do now."

"Jelisa, what do you mean you didn't want me to overreact? That bastard raped you, and you don't think I should overreact?"

"Shawnie, keep your voice down," Jelisa grunted, seeing that they were starting to draw stares.

Shawnie leaned in and looked her dead in the eyes, saying, "This goofy is lucky to even be alive right now. Not only that, but you haven't told

Shamar about it, and you got this man stalking and creeping around you and Mya. You know Shamar is going to flip when he finds out."

"I know, girl, I just need to get my thoughts together first. I'm going to tell him, and I promise you one thing: Reggie is going to get what's coming to him." What Shawnie didn't know was that Jelisa was counting on Shamar's street connections to help facilitate her revenge on Reggie. Her mind was already working on a plan to take care of him. At the present time, the most important thing to her was taking care of Mya and figuring out whether to stay married. It was becoming more than she had bargained for.

"I know this can't be easy for you, sis; but you have to remember that y'all have been through a lot and you don't want to throw it all away just because it's tough. Don't let the stuff that happened to you stop you from being able to accept when somebody is trying to love you. Shamar would kill and die for you and Mya. I would hate to see you get hurt or, better yet, you hurt him."

Shawnie's words were doing a number on Jelisa's conscience. She knew Shawnie was right. But Shawnie had no idea what it felt like, so her words only meant so much. "Look, I hear what you're saying, and I love Shamar to death. But, after all we've been through, he's left me hanging one too many times. Yeah, he was there, but he wasn't there when it mattered the most. Don't you get it? Reggie could have killed me and my daughter!" Jelisa became extremely emotional, and tears streamed from her eyes. "Where was he when this man was in my house holding my daughter? Huh? So don't give me that. I dealt with him running the streets. I put up with the shootouts, and I even brushed off the hoes trying to claim him. I let all of that go because I loved him. I can't let anything else slide. I won't do that to myself or my baby."

Shawnie reached up and wiped her little sister's tears, wishing she could take away her pain. "Jelisa, I didn't know you felt like that. I mean, I guess you have to take care of you and yours. I can't tell you how to be happy; all I can say is do what you think is best. And, real talk, I'll ride with you to take care of Reggie. Are you going to be okay?"

Jelisa nodded, saying, "I'm good. I'll take care of it. you know I always do. Just promise you will look after Mya if anything happens, all right?"

"Yeah, sis, I got you; but please don't do nothing crazy."

Nobody knew the pain and anger that was attacking Jelisa's heart. With every day that passed, she grew angrier. She had never felt this much rage. All those years of being quiet and letting stuff slide haunted her. She wasn't going to be a victim any longer.

The sisters continued to talk as they waited for their food to come. After their meal, they went on a small shopping spree before they got ready to hit the club that night.

Shamar had become distant from the rest of the people in the unit and everybody could tell something was up with him. He was usually the life of the party; but, as of late, he simply went to work, went to eat, and spent most of his time working out. He had spoken to Jelisa only once since he made it back, and it was a very dull conversation. Shamar could tell they were growing apart. Had he been able to prevent it, he would have never let her go back to Michigan City.

Shamar was just getting back from his evening workout when he stopped by the cafeteria for a snack. Lo and behold, standing a few feet in front of him was Tamika. Shamar hurried through the line to catch up with her.

"Hey. Psst. Mika, hold up."

Tamika turned around, slightly irritated with how he was calling her. But it passed when she realized it was him. "Boy, I was about to say . . .

What's up?" They gave each other a side hug and walked together to a nearby table.

"What you been up to, Mika?" Shamar asked, smiling for the first time in weeks.

Tamika offered a smile and responded, "Nothing much; I'm just passing through on my way home for a few weeks. What about you?"

"Oh, straight up? I just got back from MC a couple months ago," he said.

"Yeah, I haven't been home in a while. So when my unit gave me the chance to go, I took it. It'll be nice to get away from this for a while. How was it when you went home?" Mika asked.

Shamar's smile was immediately erased from his face.

"What's wrong?" she inquired.

"Man, my trip was hella bogus, for real. It was nothing but drama the whole time I was there. Believe it or not, I couldn't wait to leave. You remember my partna, Kaduwey?"

"You talking about the one with the dreads and the golds you used to hang with?"

"Yeah. Homie got gunned down right in front of me like the day after I got there."

Tamika's face displayed genuine concern. "Are you serious? I'm so sorry, Shamar. Did he make it?"

Shamar took a sip from his water bottle and stared off into the distance. She knew what that meant. "Naw. My guy tried to hold on as long as he could but . . ."

"Shamar, I'm sorry about your friend. You would think we'd see more of that kind of stuff over here. It makes no sense to have to go home and see it. You doing okay?" she questioned, placing her hand on his.

Shamar looked down at her hand and then back up, meeting her eyes with his. "Yeah, I'm good. It's crazy. He was trying to tell me to do something, but I don't know what it was. I think it had something to do with Chri . . ." He caught himself before he told her too much.

She picked up on his discomfort with the subject. "What were you getting ready to say?"

"Mika, you gotta promise not to say nothing, okay?"

She nodded. "Of course, Shamar. You know me better than that."

"All right. Do you remember that chick Chrissy? That one mixed chick I used to mess with?"

"Yeah, I remember her ol' nasty self. What about her?"

"Man, I think shorty got my kid, but she won't tell me. I asked, and she keeps blowing me off, begging me to let it go."

Tamika looked confused for a moment. "Wait, that don't make sense, Shamar," she said.

"What you mean?"

Tamika continued, "Shamar, she's a dyke. You didn't know? I can't believe she even had a baby. How you end up smashing that?" Tamika joked.

Shamar was puzzled; he couldn't believe what he was hearing. "Mika, stop playing, man. That broad straight up had a whole baby on me and swears up and down it ain't mine. Now you telling me she don't even like dudes. That's crazy."

"I'm pretty sure she's a carpet muncher. I told you back then you needed to be careful. Hardhead."

"Yeah, okay. But, look, do me a favor. Check in on her while you home. I need to figure out how I can get her to agree to a paternity test. I mean, I have two options. If she gets state assistance, it's mandatory that she submit to one. If not, though, I'm going to have to take her to court; and that's going to be hard to do without my wife knowing."

Tamika shook her head in disbelief. "Shamar, you didn't tell your wife about this? Boy, are you stupid? You know how females are at home; you better hope she doesn't already know. She might be plotting on you." She laughed.

"Mika, don't play like that, for real. I need to get the issue under control before I go crazy. I can't have her walking around like everything is sweet, knowing that little girl might be mine. You know I don't play like that."

Trying to stop laughing at his desperation, Tamika agreed. "Okay, I'll see what I can do. Now, what's your wife's name again? Jelisa, right?"

"Yeah, you know her. We went to school with her sister Shawnie."

"Yeah, I remember. Boy, you sure know how to pick 'em. Look, I need to get out of here. I'm flying out tomorrow night, and you know how that is. So I'll see you later. Give me a call in a few days. Here's my number in case you lost it." Tamika stood up after writing her number on a piece of paper and handing it to him. They shared a friendly embrace and parted ways.

Shamar grabbed his snack and returned to his quarters, feeling more confused than he did before their conversation. *What the hell did I get myself into with this chick? I swear I can't let Jelisa find out about this. Ain't no way she's going to believe this,* he thought as he walked out.

***

Tamika arrived in Michigan City a couple days later, after a couple of false starts at the airports. Tuesday nights were usually boring in the city; the only people out were crackheads, D-boys, and hoes. She made it to the east side, where her parents lived, and figured she'd recover and stay in for the night.

The next morning, she went over to Platinum Designs to get her eyebrows done and to speak with Donny. He had always been like a big brother to her. Their families grew up together on Emily Street. She entered the shop that morning only planning to catch up with Donny and, hopefully, get the scoop on Chrissy.

"I'm saying, though, I take off for a few years, and my big bro don't even try to keep in touch," Tamika said jokingly, mimicking Donny's trademark walk and voice.

Donny, who was sitting in his barber chair, cleaning his clippers, recognized her voice and his face lit up. Pushing himself out of his seat, his eyes beamed with excitement as he called out to her, "Oh, word? Don't do me like that, Mika. What's good with you? When you get back? Look at you, Miss Soldier."

"Big head, you ain't changed at all, have you? I see you still got the shop up and running. I just got back from Iraq. They let me come home for a few weeks before I go to my next unit. How's everything going?" Tamika asked, reaching out for a hug. They embraced and walked back over to Donny's station, where she sat down in his chair.

"Can you hook my eyebrows up for me? I'm woofin' right now," she said, examining her face in the mirror behind him.

"Yeah, I got you. Things have been straight around here, you know. I'm eatin'. I saw your mom the other day, and I told her to tell you I said hi."

Tamika smirked, looking at Donny's reflection and saying, "Yeah, right, boy. Stop lying. You ain't bit more seen my mama. She don't even leave the house anymore."

"Yeah, you got me. But, anyway, what you been up to?"

As she looked around the shop admiring the décor, Tamika noticed a picture of Shamar and Jelisa by her workstation. She had no idea that Jelisa worked in Donny's shop. "Jelisa works here? When she start working over here?"

Donny looked over at the picture and rolled his eyes. Noticing his frustration, Tamika asked, "What's wrong with you? What, you don't like her or something? I mean, you are taking her booth rent. Why hire her if you don't like her?"

Donny answered, "Naw, it's nothing like that. She's just too much of a live wire. Plus, me and her dude don't get along. But she knows how to bring in that money."

"Yeah, I feel that. It is what it is, I guess. Donny, do you remember Chrissy? That one mixed chick from the west side who used to mess with them chicks from LaPorte?"

Donny thought for a second and remembered who she was talking about. "Oh, yeah. You talking 'bout shorty with the little girl? Yeah, I remember her. She be running round her burning people and whatnot. I was surprised that everybody didn't know she liked chicks. People still act surprised when they hear about it. Why you ask?"

Not wanting to give it away, Tamika thought fast and answered, "No reason. I'm just being nosy. I saw her earlier this morning while I was on my way here. That's all, no biggie."

"Oh, okay, I guess. That chick is bad news anyways. You not playing for the rainbow team are you?" he asked.

"Boy, go on somewhere with that. Don't even play with me like that."

Donny smiled as if he didn't really believe her. "So how long are you home for?"

"I'm on leave for four weeks, and then I'm headed to Georgia. But after I leave here, I'm going to have lunch with my sister and hang out for a while."

Donny, being a typical creep, viewed this as a chance to get at Tamika. A girl like her being overseas for months had to be in need of a good pounding. "All right, well, holla at me when you get some free time. We need to kick it."

Tamika, not at all wise to his insinuation, smiled and agreed. "Yeah, we can do that. Just write your number down, and I'll hit you up later."

After Donny had finished with her, he wouldn't let her pay. He was good with the fact that she agreed to hook up. Donny wrote down his number on the back of a business card, and Tamika gave him hers. They shared a brief hug, and she bid him good-bye. Donny watched with lust in his eyes as Tamika walked out of the shop, unknowingly tempting him with every step.

She done got thick as hell. I'm definitely smashing. Tamika drove off, headed to her sister's house, while Donny went back to his normal activities.

Chapter Fourteen

While he was locked up, Block once had a
man tell him that every black man in America
has experienced some form of racism or another.
He had never experienced it until he entered the
department of corrections. He couldn't believe
the amount of confidence this so-called brotha
exhibited when he made that statement. Block's
thoughts? *Another typical nigga trying to
blame white people for black people's problems.*
Let him tell it, that type of attitude always
pissed him off. Block hated to hear people talk
like that. As he sat in the great room of his new
home, he turned on the fifty-inch flat-screen
TV and turned to the local news. Being away
for so long only granted him the opportunity to
know what was going on on the outside through
newspaper and the prison grapevine. He grew
up believing that as long as the motives behind
his actions were righteous, justice would always
be on his side. Unlike many people his age

growing up in Michigan City, Block didn't know what it was like to be profiled by the police or be followed around in a department store. The fact was he had only seen and heard of examples of racism and prejudice.

As the news reporter came on, a picture of an old white lady and a beat-up Crown Victoria flashed on the screen. She reported that the woman had blown through a red light while making a right-hand turn. Not paying attention to where she was going she mowed down eight-year-old Naomi Taylor and her fourteen-year-old brother Justin. Unfortunately, after she lay up in the children's hospital for almost two weeks, baby girl didn't survive. The reporter stated that the community was outraged, especially when the white woman got off with probation and a suspended license.

Block could feel the rage building up inside as he listened to the news anchor revisit the events that had taken place surrounding this injustice. It was stated that not long after that incident a middle-aged black woman found herself in the same situation and she was given fifteen years for manslaughter.

Hearing this news was starting to ruin Block's mood so he quickly turned off the TV and went into the bedroom to prepare for whatever it was that Toya had planned for him that night. After getting dressed, he stepped out to take a brief ride around town. He had been locked up long enough, and he wasn't interested in being stuck in his bedroom all day.

Tamika and her mother had just returned from a brief shopping spree at the Prime Outlets on the west side. After she had helped her mother into the house, she went back outside to finish unloading the rest of her bags. The pounding and vibration of subwoofers made her car rattle. She turned around to see a cocaine white Chevy Caprice approaching her from behind. The windows were blacked out, and the smell of weed escaped from the slightly opened windows. Her combat instincts were beginning to kick in; and, just then, a tall, light-skinned goon appeared from the car. Donning an Indiana Pacers fitted cap with the brim covering his eyes, he flashed his pearly whites behind his bushy goatee. Tamika tossed her bags back into the trunk and faced the man's car head-on.

"What's good, mama? How you come home and not hit Block up, Mika?"

Tamika's mind struggled to match the face to the voice. It sounded so familiar, but she couldn't place the face.

"Why you staring like you don't know me no more? I know it ain't been that long." He laughed.

When he laughed, it dawned on her that it was her old friend Dee Block from the west side. She let her guard down immediately and a big smile shined on her face. He opened his arms and motioned with his head for her to come and give him a hug.

"Block, you better stop rolling up on people like that. You 'bout gave me a heart attack," she said as they separated. She punched him on the arm and smirked, thankful that he wasn't a jump-out boy. They were known for sticking up females as well as guys, especially those driving cars with out-of-town plates.

"Aww, shorty, you know it ain't like that."

"What you been up to? I see you still stuntin' like usual."

Block had been a career criminal since he was fourteen. He, Shamar, and Kaduwey were a force to be reckoned with when they hit the block. Block stayed behind when Shamar went off to the Army, and he had always seemed to miss the chance to see him when he was home. Block grinned and responded, "You know me, Mika; I stay moving, getting this money and pimping these hoes. Hell, I'm fresh out the DOC. I hate I missed my boy Shamar when he was here. I got jammed up for a second with my parole officer and got stuck out of town when I heard about Kaduwey. I swear I did everything I could to get back here, but they had me sitting for a minute while my paperwork got checked out. That's why when I heard you were here, I had to come holla at you before you left. Why don't you let me take you out so we can catch up?"

"When you talking?"

"We can go right now. You know me; I don't make no plans. Go run your stuff in the crib and we can shoot over to Merrillville real fast."

Tamika smiled, seductively biting down on her finger, and said, "All right. I'll be right back." She popped the trunk, grabbed the last of her bags, and trotted up the sidewalk into the house. A few minutes later, she reappeared from the house.

They got into Block's car and took off down the road. Block hadn't lost his touch. He still had it, and he knew Tamika had a thing for him. There was no telling with him; anything was likely to happen tonight. But she was happy to be along for the ride.

***

Three hours and a few thousand dollars later, Block had been successful at solidifying his place in Tamika's heart. It didn't take long for them to end up at one of Block's favorite spots back in the city, the Blue Chip Casino. They had dinner and capped off their evening in Block's favorite part of the riverboat experience: a luxury suite, which was one that he often used as the final destination for special occasions with his select dimes.

When they arrived at their room, Block ordered hors d'oeuvres and drinks to be brought up to the room. The two didn't do much eating; but, after an hour, they had gone through a bottle of Rémy Martin, and they both were buzzed. As they reclined on the bed, Tamika straddled Block and stared into his eyes, drunk with lust. With her hands on his chest, bracing herself, she slowly ground on him, making him hard as a rock.

"Baby, you gon' keep teasing me or you gon' put some work in? You know I've been waiting a long time now to break you off. Tell Block what's good," Block flirted, cupping her perky breasts with his huge hands.

"Ooh, daddy, I've been wanting it too," Tamika moaned, licking and biting her bottom lip. She slid back, placing herself between his legs and kneeling in front of his swollen member.

Block leaned forward, admiring her seductive eyes staring back at him. He nodded with approval, slightly drunk himself. She unzipped his jeans and went to work.

An hour and a half later, they both lay drunk and sweaty as they tried to recover from their sexual excursion. They both showered and lay together on the bed, watching TV. Tamika lay naked on top of Block, drawing circles on his chest with her finger.

She gazed into his eyes and Block asked, "Shorty, what's on your mind? Why you staring at me like that?"

"Nothing, it's just . . ." She paused, not wanting to ruin the mood.

"What's good? Just say it; ain't no need to be all quiet now. What's on your mind? You know Block got all the answers." He smiled, reassuring her.

"Okay. You remember how tight you were with Shamar, right?"

Block grinned. "Yeah, no doubt. That's my guy right there. What's up? He in trouble or something?"

Tamika shook her head and replied, "Not really. He told me something about this chick Chrissy supposedly having his baby or something, but she not claiming him. I told him I would ask around while I was here to kind of help him out."

Block nodded again, and his eyes indicated he was searching his mind for any information he might have come across. Block's eyes lit up like he had just thought of the world's greatest idea.

"What?" Tamika asked.

"Yeah, I know Chrissy. As a matter of fact, I was thinking about the one time, like a week ago, when we were at this party at O'Reilly's. Me and shorty ended up at one of my spots drunk as hell." Block smiled as he played back the events in his mind. "You know the saying, 'A drunk man tells no tales?' Well, this was a prime example of that. Shorty was so lit she started pouring out all kinds of secrets, and I'm pretty sure she doesn't remember any of it. But, anyway, I do remember her saying something about her not ever telling him about the baby because it would ruin everything. Now, I don't know what she meant by that; but, from what I know about her, that meant she did something shiesty."

As Tamika processed what Block told her, she became slightly irritated. "That's jacked up. Here we got all these females who complain about not having their kids' fathers around, and she pulls something like that. That ain't right."

"Aww, don't worry about that, shorty. It's all good. Shamar can handle it. I wouldn't worry too much about it. But, anyway, you ready for round two?" Block said, smacking her on the butt.

She smiled and moaned, climbing back on top of him, ready to put in more work. Their night of passion lasted a couple more hours until they both were left exhausted. The lovers slept in each other's arms, not waking until check-out time the next morning. As they enjoyed breakfast together, Block caught a glimpse of Tamika staring out the window.

"What's up, mama? What's on your mind?"

"I don't know, Block. I just hate seeing good dudes get played by these no-good females. You know Shamar is like my brother. I can't let that happen to him. Can you help me with something?"

Block nodded his head, wishing that he wouldn't have said anything in the first place. But he had love for Tamika so whatever she wanted she only needed to ask. "You know I got you. Shamar's my brother anyway, and you know how I feel about these deadbeat hoes. What's the play?"

"I just need to find out where she hangs at. I know she used to live on the east side. I ain't trying to stalk her or nothing; I just want to get a look at the little girl and see what Chrissy's been up to."

Block was amused by Tamika's sudden passion for justice. "Girl, you about to turn into the feds, huh? You better be careful; you know Chrissy got a thing for chicks too. I got you, though. Just give me until tonight. I'll have a line on her."

Tamika nodded and grinned, saying, "Thank you, baby. You always look out for me. Thank you for last night, too. You know how to make a girl feel special." She got up from her seat and strutted past him seductively in her bra and panties.

Block reached over and pulled her to him, sitting her on his lap. He winked at her and kissed her on the cheek. "You know Block got you. It's all good."

After they checked out, Block took Tamika back to her mother's house. He helped her with her bags, and they hugged and kissed, bidding each other good-bye. Just as she made it to her front porch, she looked back to wave at Block, only to see Donny driving past slowly. He looked at Block, then at her, and smirked.

Block blew him off and looked back at Tamika, saying, "Hey, shorty, you good? Do I need to take care of him?"

"Naw, I'm good, Block. Thanks, baby. Call me later."

Tamika went into the house as Block sped off down the road. Neither paid Donny any mind; however, Tamika found it strange that he would come by her house almost as if he was checking on her. Her instincts were kicking in, and she knew she would have to watch her back with him for the rest of the time she was home.

Chapter Fifteen

Shamar had finally begun to readjust to being back in Iraq, and he had been trying to reach Jelisa for days. He knew she was probably busy and still upset with him. It wasn't out of the ordinary for her to avoid him when she was mad. It left him feeling helpless being so far away with no other option but to wait.

After a late-night workout, Shamar headed to the phone center with high hopes that he would finally get a chance to talk to Jelisa and Mya. He could never get used to not being able to hear his baby girl's voice. As the phone rang, Shamar rehearsed the conversation, carefully choosing his words.

"Hello?" Jelisa answered. There were voices in the background at the restaurant they were eating at.

"What's up, sweetheart?"

"Hey, Shamar," she said, unenthused.

"You don't sound happy to hear from me. What's going on? I've been trying to reach you for days." Shamar tried to mask his frustration as he awaited her response.

"Shamar, I'm not trying to go there with you. You know I'm happy to hear from you. I'm in Indianapolis with Shawnie, and the reception is bad at our hotel; that's why you couldn't reach me. It's not like I can just pick up and call you," she said with an attitude.

"Hmm. Where is Mya, with your mom?"

"Yes, Shamar."

He fought the urge to pop off, and replied, "Jelisa, what is wrong with you? Why are you being so short with me?"

Jelisa wasn't interested in talking with Shamar; she was too busy enjoying her time with Shawnie. "Look, Shamar, I'm not trying to be short with you; I just don't have anything to talk about. I mean, I miss you and all but it's not like I can just come see you, so there's no need to get my hopes up. I'll talk you when I get some free time. Bye."

Shamar was furious. He couldn't believe she had the audacity to hang up on him. *This broad done lost her mind, boy. I* . . . He didn't even bother to call back. He knew if she hung up again, or didn't pick up, there was nothing he could do but be mad. He slammed the phone down on the hook and stormed out.

"Man, I can't deal with this right now. That girl is going to make me hurt somebody. I can't believe this," Shamar said to himself as he walked back to camp.

This was a blow to Shamar as it left him questioning if they were going to make it through the rest of his deployment. As many marriages as he had seen fall apart because of deployments, he worried more than he ever had before. At this point, he had to figure out how he could keep his marriage from falling apart from thousands of miles away. The only person he could call on was Pete, and he knew it was a long shot because he never interfered in their business. It was something he had to do, no matter how uncomfortable it would be.

The next evening, after another intense workout and a bout with himself to work up the nerve to call Pete, Shamar caved. His breathing became shallow as the phone began to ring. Shamar had seen and experienced everything the streets had thrown at him, yet here he was nervous at the thought of speaking to Pete.

"Hello? Who is this?" Pete said, clearing his throat.

"Hello, sir, this is Shamar. I need to talk to you."

"Hey there, young man, how are you? Keeping safe, I hope."

"Yes, sir, I'm fine for the most part. I just . . ."

"What's on your mind? I can tell something is off. I can hear it in your voice. You and my daughter hit another rough patch?"

Shamar tried to keep from breaking down, but the more he spoke, the more his voice trembled. "I don't know what to do with her, sir. I'm stuck over here, and there's nothing I can do. I feel like I'm losing her, sir; and I'm going crazy over here." Shamar knees bounced up and down repeatedly under the table in the booth he sat in.

"Calm yourself down, son; it's going to be okay. Now you know I don't usually get involved in my daughter's affairs, but if I had any reason to believe Jelisa was in danger, I would do something. But as far as this is concerned, you need to keep fighting for your marriage. You can only do so much, son. So if my daughter decides being married isn't something she can handle, you have to decide what you want to do."

Shamar didn't want to hear that. The thought of losing her drove him crazy. "Come on, sir, don't say that. You know I love Jelisa. I'd do anything for her."

"Would you let her go if that's what she wanted? I mean, if she really pushed the issue and

wanted out. You know these women are fin-
icky creatures, and trust me when I say Jelisa
is her mother's daughter. So don't underesti-
mate her."

What Pete was saying was disheartening and
unfortunately very true. Shamar knew that
Jelisa was a strong-willed person and once her
mind was made up to do something that was
it. The only problem was, even though Shamar
had his fair share of women who came and went,
even while they were together, he never really
cheated in his opinion. Maybe a blowjob here
and there, but nothing that could tie him to
anyone. Shamar wasn't prepared to take a loss
like that, but his pride was beginning to harden
his heart. If he had to let Jelisa go, the only thing
that would make it impossible was not being
able to see Mya. He wasn't about to let her or any
woman get the best of him.

Shamar once thought of himself as Jelisa's
best friend, but he was still from the streets.
After all they had been through, and the way she
was acting, losing her wasn't the worst thing in
the world at this point.

"Look, sir, I feel what you're saying, and I don't
want to lose her, but I've never been one to beg
any woman for anything. So if she ain't feeling
this anymore, it is what it is. I'm just tired, sir.

Why doesn't she just tell me she wants out?" Shamar felt himself getting ready to cry. As he swallowed the lump in his throat, he considered the idea of not having Jelisa in his life. "Look, sir, I'm not going to front like I don't care about her leaving; I obviously do because I called. I just don't know where I went wrong. I just—"

Pete interrupted Shamar, sensing that he was becoming overwhelmed. "Son, son, listen to me. As men, we all make mistakes. As a husband, you will never do everything right; you just have to do your best to take care of your family. I know it's hard to accept, but you can't make a woman do anything she doesn't want to do without pushing her away. So you just keep doing what you're doing, pray for your family, and make it home to them in one piece. You hear me?"

Shamar could only take what Pete was saying for what it was: truth. There was nothing he could do but wait and pray, which was something he hadn't done in a long time. "You're right, sir; I guess that's all I can do." Shamar paused and took in a deep breath. He sighed and continued, "Well, sir, I really appreciate you talking to me. I don't have anybody else to turn to. But I need to let you go. I have a couple other things to take care of before I lie down. It's getting pretty late over here."

"All right, son. Don't hesitate to give me a call if you need something. I'm here."

"Yes, sir, talk to you soon. Bye." After hanging up with Pete, Shamar was left with a lot to think about. Everything he had done seemed to have come full circle. Karma was about to get busy if he didn't figure something out.

As the weeks passed, conversations between Shamar and Jelisa became fewer and shorter. Jelisa almost sounded like she had moved on from him. Most of the time, they would talk just long enough for Shamar to talk to Mya. Their conversations were empty and shallow, which pushed them further apart.

He had never gotten a chance to catch up with Tamika when she was home. As far as he knew, Chrissy was now a liability; and that added to the stress of being away. The more Shamar thought about it, he wondered if it was possible that Jelisa knew about Chrissy and her daughter. This could explain why she was suddenly so standoffish with him. It didn't make sense, though, because knowing Jelisa, that was definitely not something she would keep quiet about. Only time would tell just how damaged their relationship really was.

Chapter Sixteen

Last night was a hell of a night. I think I cleared about five thousand and them thirsty niggas was tricking off their whole paychecks. I know there's some goofy female at home with a bunch of kids wondering where her baby daddy is, Christina Michaels thought. She stood in front of her dresser, staring at her mirror, examining the bags under her eyes.

Unfortunately for the wives and girlfriends of her primary investors, Chrissy didn't feel sorry for any of them. She thought they ought to know better than to let their men run the streets that late at night anyway. "I wish my man would let me catch him in one of these trashy clubs and I'm not with him," she spoke to her reflection.

She never liked that white girl name her mother had given her, so she started going by Chrissy to take the awkwardness away. Hearing her explain her come up from the night before would lead most to believe she was in a strip club popping her thang for a little piece of change. Not at all; Chrissy had a few niggas who owed her favors here and there, but the hoes at the clubs all broke her off a piece of everything they made.

The thirty-three-year-old beauty looked to be no older than twenty. She was a silent partner for this hole-in-the-wall strip club on the south side of Chicago called Shelly's. The owner was one of her homegirls from way back who found herself getting shaken down by some local wannabe thugs. In response, Chrissy took it upon herself to put in some work for her dear friend. In return, she cut her in on part of the profit.

Truth be told Chrissy was heartless and that came from seeing a man die in front of her when she was younger. The trauma from witnessing that led to her choosing drugs over everything else. Every now and then she wished that one of these days that man would come knocking on her door or she'd run into him on the street. That would lift the burden that she had carried for over fifteen years.

"After a long night of partying, I swear with the headache I have this morning, I will never drink again," Chrissy said to herself as the sun beamed through the blinds of her bedroom window. She got up to jump in the shower and realized she had thrown up all over her Coach sneakers. "I can't believe this. I just got these shoes yesterday," she said to herself, tiptoeing to the bathroom.

The self-proclaimed hustler had a habit of overdoing it when she drank anything with vodka in it. The night prior was her girl Tisha's twenty-fifth birthday, and they went all in. There were a bunch of thirsty niggas who were salty that they had shown them up and bought out the bar for their entourage. And, of course, you had the hating hoes who could only wish they were in their shoes. After about an hour Chrissy began to have a feeling one of them was watching her kind of hard and usually when she got that feeling something always popped off. Just to be safe, she slowed down on the shots so she wouldn't give anybody the upper hand in case they tried something.

There had to be at least twenty of her girls on one side of the club; it was thick. Tisha and Chrissy slid off to the bathroom for a quick fix. She didn't think anybody would have noticed them sneak off. She had a bit of an affair with what some call "nose candy." In her opinion, she was no cokehead or anything; she just used it to take the edge off when she was trying to get nice. After a couple lines, they emerged from the bathroom, when Chrissy noticed that same ho from earlier with her hand on her brand new Michael Kors handbag.

"Tisha, please tell me this ho does not have her funky little hands on my bag. I'm about to beat the hell out of her," she said, going straight from zero to ten.

Chrissy rushed over and without breaking stride grabbed her by her cheap, kinky twists and dragged her all the way to the dance floor. The next thing you knew, there were five of her friends along with her on the woman. Chrissy was trying her hardest to snatch every braid out of her head.

After the fight was broken up the woman who was jumped got thrown out of the club, and Chrissy and her entourage continued to pour up. In spite of the fallout, the night ended as well as it started and Chrissy went to bed feeling like she was at the top of the world. She knew the next morning was likely to be a rough one. Chrissy was set to meet with her probation officer for her final check-in before she would finally be off papers.

Block was on the boulevard grabbing something to eat when Toya called. "I'm at my condo.

Why don't you come over now? I've got some business to talk to you about. I'm over by the beach. Just call me when you're close, and I'll give you directions," she said, trying to mask the excitement about what she was planning for him.

Block made a U-turn at the light near Carrol Avenue and headed back toward downtown. "Yeah, I can do that. I need to stop at the Duke to pick up some Black & Milds real quick."

As he turned into the entrance of the gas station, memories from his childhood flashed through his mind. He had thoughts of hanging out in front of the store, watching the gangsters and hustlers parade their new cars and shoot dice on the side of the building. A grin emerged on his face as he parked. Suddenly, he noticed a woman walking in front of his truck toward one of the pumps. "What the hell? I know that ain't . . . Is that?" Block said, rolling down the dark-tinted window on his driver's side.

It was hard for him to tell if he recognized this stunning young lady. As she turned and looked over her shoulder, Block did recognize her. She faintly resembled Chrissy, the girl Shamar stressed out. He hadn't seen her in years, but the resemblance was not enough to convince him it was her. As he further investigated, it was clear he had seen her before. She was the rude woman who nearly knocked him over at the courthouse. Part of him wanted to cuss her out for being so rude but fifteen years behind those walls made her quite the prize. Disregarding his desire for tobacco, Block climbed out of his truck and took the quickest route to engage the voluptuous woman. "Say, sweetheart, what's good? Can I talk to you for a second?" he said, strutting his way in between cars.

The young lady stopped and spun around full of arrogance, only to be shocked at the sight of the man standing before her. Her heart started beating rapidly, and her knees got weak. She stuttered, "Hey, um, what's up? You talking to me?"

She looked nervous and for a second Block wondered if he had been too aggressive with his approach. It had been quite some time since he had to put his gift of gab to use. He responded cunningly, "Yeah, how you doing? Do I know you from somewhere? You kind of look familiar. What's your name?"

She wasn't sure what to say as she held a secret he had yet to discover; and, since he didn't know who she was, she took that as a way out. She knew how tight he and Shamar were and having heard he was in town she knew he wouldn't be far behind. She did not know that

Shamar had already gone back. She responded sharply, "Yeah, I don't think that's a good idea. I've got to go."

Caught off guard Block scrambled to salvage the encounter. "Wait a minute, shorty. What's wrong? Where you going?" he said, gently grabbing her hand.

"Boy, if you don't let me go!" she snapped.

Block's face twisted in shock as her voice changed and sounded familiar. "What the hell? Chrissy, is that you? Come here!" he shouted as she slipped from his grip.

She jumped in her car and locked the doors before speeding out of the parking lot. Block rushed back to his truck and attempted to catch up with her. As they both raced down the boulevard back toward the east side, Block's mind raced, trying to figure out what had just happened. Why did Chrissy look so different, and what was she hiding? He hadn't seen her in years, and it seemed like she'd aged quite a bit. It didn't make any sense for her to behave this way after all this time. He had to find out and soon.

As Chrissy sped down the boulevard, she was still overcome with shock. The only thing she could think of was getting the hell out of Michigan City. She took the nearest exit to get to Interstate 94. As she headed west toward

Chicago, she could see Block's truck in her rear-view mirror swerving in and out of traffic. "Oh my God, why is this happening to me? Where the hell did he come from and why is he back here? I have to get away from here."

As the high-speed chase ensued, police joined in as well. Block couldn't believe he had allowed himself to get caught up in this mess over nothing. As he considered the possible outcome of this situation he determined it wasn't worth it at all.

When he hit his brakes to slow down and hop off the nearest exit, his truck hit a pothole, causing him to lose control. He swerved and struggled to regain control, but he was going too fast. In a last-minute effort to save himself, Block grabbed his seat belt, which he had failed to put on. The vehicle spun around and tumbled, rolling across the interstate. The truck came to a stop, and Block was thrown through the windshield into the grass on the side of the road.

Eventually, he was taken by ambulance to the nearest hospital, where he surprisingly only suffered a broken arm and a few scratches. It seemed the grass cushioned the impact when he landed.

He spent a week in recovery before being released. He managed to smooth things over with his parole officer after convincing him that an unknown driver ran him off the road. He was good at talking his way out of stuff when it mattered.

As Shamar packed up his things to prepare to return to the States, his heart was heavy. He hadn't spoken to Jelisa in over a month, and she had no idea he was coming home. Unsure of how to stage his return, Shamar reached out to Tamika through e-mail. She had relocated to the Army in-processing center in Chicago, instead of Georgia, which allowed her to be closer to home. They arranged to meet up once he was settled back in Fort Riley.

Shamar's unit made it back home just as the fall weather was beginning to change the color of the leaves on the trees. He hadn't realized how much he missed the smell of fresh air after smelling nothing but gunpowder and raw sewage for so long.

Shamar flew into Chicago to meet Tamika and Block. As he made his way from baggage claim, he could see the two of them waiting by the sliding door that led out to the parking garage. Block stood leaning up against his Chevy, which was fresh out of the detail shop. Tamika stood in front of him, wrapping herself in his arms and smiling.

Block looked up and nodded at him. "What's good, soldier boy? How was the trip?" The two shook hands, embraced briefly, and shared a laugh.

Shamar smiled and answered, "What's good, Block? How long has it been? I see you and Mika been getting it in." He looked over at Tamika, who was now three months pregnant and glowing. Tamika smiled and rubbed her stomach.

"You know how I do, bruh. Mika, pop the trunk for me, would you?" Block said as he helped Shamar with his luggage. Once everything was loaded, Block helped Tamika into the back seat while he and Shamar sat in the front.

As they hit the highway, Shamar stared out the window, contemplating what he might be going home to. Block tapped him on his arm, disrupting his daydream. "Hey, Shamar. Shamar? So what's the deal, man? How's Jelisa doing? I've been seeing her out a lot lately. Y'all all right?"

Shamar looked over with a look of confusion and irritation on his face. "Man, I don't know, fam. We not even really talking right now. I haven't heard from her in a minute, and she don't even know I'm home. I guess we'll see when we get to the city, huh?"

Block nodded and looked at Tamika in the review mirror as if he was getting permission for something. She nodded as well and Block glanced over at Shamar. "Say, homie, what's the deal with Chrissy?"

Shamar wasn't expecting that topic to come up so soon. He shook his head, loathing the idea of even talking about it. Looking into the side-view mirror, he replied, "Fam, that's a whole different situation. I don't know what I'm going to do about that one."

"I know what you mean, man. That ho crazy as hell. But, I will tell you that shorty look just like you. It's wild that she's acting like that, though, 'cause that white boy she's with is dumb as hell for staying with her. He believes everything she tells him."

"I know him, and I can't believe he is dumb enough to believe her either; but I'm going to get answers one way or another."

The last few months had been eye-opening for Jelisa. In spite of the advice Shawnie gave her, she chose to do her own thing. She and Donny had been kicking tough, and Shamar was the last thing on her mind. Numb to the fact that she was still married and clueless about Shamar being home, Jelisa was reckless. She and Donny didn't hide the fact that they were creeping.

As Jelisa was finishing up with a client, she and Donny traded smiles from across the room. Jelisa's cell rang, and an unknown number popped up on her caller ID. She shook her head and excused herself to the back room.

"Hello? Hello?" she said, but there was no answer on the other end.

Just as she was about to hang up, a man's voice whispered, "Hey, sweetheart, so you ready to handle our little bit of business or what?"

Jelisa hesitated as she tried to familiarize herself with the voice. At first, she thought it was Shamar, and her attitude was about to kick in until he spoke again.

"You know, I don't think ol' soldier boy would appreciate the extracurricular activities you've been participating in."

Suddenly, it dawned on her. It wasn't Shamar; it was Reggie. Her heart sank, and she was filled with anxiety. Her voice quivered as she responded, "Reggie, I thought I told you to leave me the hell alone," she whispered, trying not to attract attention to herself. "Reggie, what do you want?"

He let out a sinister laugh and answered, "You know what I want, angel. Now we can do this the easy way, or I can introduce our little princess to some of my favorite games. You know how I like playing games."

Jelisa immediately became furious. She paced back and forth in the back room, her hands shaking and her stomach in knots. "You listen to me, ain't nobody playing with you! If you go anywhere near my daughter, I'll slit your throat myself."

Reggie laughed as Jelisa fumed on the other end of the line. He continued to toy with her. "Yo, angel, I thought you knew me better than that. Let's not make idle threats. I'm sure you want me dead. But, let's face it, you can never get rid of me. I'm in your head, and you'll never let me go."

Jelisa was repulsed by his conceit. She snapped back at him, "Screw you, Reggie! I swear to God I will kill you if you come near me or my family!" she shouted.

"You know you are wearing the hell out of that skirt today, angel. My, you really have developed quite nicely."

Jelisa's eyes widened, and a chill ran down her spine. She slowly moved from the back area to the front and peered around the corner to look out of the shop windows. Outside, Reggie sat in his Cadillac, smiling and blowing cigar smoke out the window.

"You have three days, angel, three days. I'll be in touch. I know where to find you," Reggie said as he sped off.

As the sound of tires screeching filled the air, Jelisa was overcome with panic and worry. She slowly put her phone in her pocket and lowered her head in shame. She couldn't believe what Reggie was trying to do to her. Where was Shamar when she needed him? Nowhere to be found; but, this time, it wasn't his fault. She had cut him off and pushed him away. Even if he couldn't be there with her, she knew he had enough pull to at least make a call on her behalf. With Reggie back in the picture, she needed to be able to count on his pull to get him away from her. Jelisa knew Donny wasn't the type who could hold her down if it came to some street politics. She disappeared into the back again to gather herself.

Donny noticed that she looked flustered but he withheld his comments, thinking she might have gotten into it with Shamar. That, of course, would have been great news for him. Minutes later, Jelisa emerged from the back, apologizing to her client for the interruption.

***

As they made it into the city limits, Block looked over at Shamar, wondering what was going through his mind. "Shamar, what's good, bro? Where you want me to drop you?"

Shamar thought about it and, not wanting to be caught off guard himself by popping up at Donny's shop, he replied, "Take me by Wey's crib so I can pick up my car from Ashley. I got some things to figure out before I go holla at Jelisa."

"All right, man, I got you," Block said, looking back at Tamika, who was fast asleep in the back.

When they pulled up to Kaduwey's house, Ashley was waiting in the doorway. After helping Shamar with his bags, Block shook hands with him and gave him a brief embrace. "Hey, homie, hit me up tomorrow; let's catch up some more. If you need anything, holla at me. I got you. You feel me?"

"Yeah, Block. I appreciate it, man. I'll hit you once I get settled. Love, bruh. Tell Mika I said I'll talk to her later."

Block drove off as Shamar headed up the driveway to the house. When she let him into the house, Ashley greeted him with a warm hug. As they separated, she had tears in her eyes. She hadn't seen him since the day he came to the hospital. Seeing his face flooded her mind with thoughts of Kaduwey, and her heart filled with grief.

"Ash, come on, sweetheart. Don't cry, ma. It's all right. Come sit down," he said, helping her to her seat. "So how you been holding up, Ash? I can tell it's still hard for you."

Ashley wiped her face and cleared her throat. She looked over at him with her big brown eyes and replied, "It has been hard. I'm not even going to lie. Everybody's been helping out, though. I just can't get used to him not being here. What am I going to do?" She began weeping again, and all Shamar could do was hold her and attempt to comfort her.

After a few minutes, Ashley finally calmed down. She gave him an endearing gaze and reached over and grabbed his hand. "Shamar, I don't know how to tell you this because I don't want to hurt your feelings."

"What's up?" Shamar knew it was probably something about Jelisa. He knew it wouldn't be long before people started getting at him about her.

"You know I don't normally get in people's business, especially when it comes to relationships. I mean, you were there for my baby when nobody else was, and you been looking out for us as well. You're like my big brother, so I have to tell you that Jelisa's been wildin' out since you left the last time. It's like she ain't even trying to hide it. Does she know you're home?"

Shamar wasn't surprised; he had long suspected her heart was gone. As much as it hurt, he was cool as long as Mya was okay. But one thing was for sure, he wasn't going to just walk away. He nodded his head and leaned back on the couch, resting his arm on the edge behind Ashley.

"I know Ash. I mean, come on; you know me. I ain't ever been the type to let any female play me. I might be a bit of a pushover when it comes to baby girl, but I'm not going to hold on to nobody when they want to go. I'm good, and she can do whatever makes her happy. Ash, honestly, I'm just tired of fighting. I understand that being apart for almost a year can ruin a relationship; so, at this point, I'm not even mad."

Ashley was amazed at his response. But as she looked deeper into his eyes, she saw through to his soul, and there lay the true hurt he was feeling. "Wow, Shamar, she really hurt you, huh?"

"Naw, not really. I've just seen so much and lost so much over the last year that I'm not going to let it bother me. So it is what it is; you know what I mean?" Shamar's nonchalant response said it all and Ashley knew his mind was set.

"So, what's next? I mean, you can stay here with me and K.D.; it would do him some good to have a man around. Plus, he knows you. He looks at that picture of you and Kaduwey every day." Hearing that put a smile on Shamar's face, leading him to agree to stay.

It was getting late, and Ashley had just put K.D. to bed. Shamar didn't realize how comfortable Ashley was around him until she walked past him in a wife beater and boy shorts. He looked on as she paraded around the house, flaunting every curve on her body. Ashley stopped in front of him and bent over, picking up K.D.'s toys. All Shamar could think about was her slipping out of her shorts and jumping on his lap.

Standing up, Ashley noticed Shamar adjusting himself in his pants. She looked at him and smiled, saying playfully, "You see something you like? I guess that year was pretty long, huh?"

Shamar grinned, slightly embarrassed, but he reminded himself that she was supposed to be like his sister. That wouldn't be a good look. "You playing, huh? Go on somewhere before you get us both in trouble," he said jokingly.

"Um hmm," Ashley said as she disappeared into her bedroom.

Shamar figured she was just feeling lonely and he didn't want to cross the line with her. He set himself up in the spare room and prepared himself for his encounter with Jelisa. He had no idea how it would go, but it had to be done.

Chapter Seventeen

"I can't believe this bastard is still after me," Jelisa said to herself as she packed up her and Mya's things.

She had to hurry and leave town before Reggie made good on his threat. There was no telling what he would do if he was going to the lengths he was to get to her. She heard a knock at the door and her heart skipped a beat. With Mya asleep in her room, Jelisa crept next to the door and grabbed her pistol out of her purse. Her mind began to panic, wondering who it might be. Cautiously, she opened the door, holding her pistol at her side. When she opened the door, Donny stood there, smiling like he had just won the lottery. She quickly tucked the pistol in the pocket of one of her jackets that was hanging on the wall behind the door.

"Donny, what are you doing here? I thought I told you about popping up unannounced. What's up?" she said, hurrying him inside.

They had been so careless lately that Donny felt less like a visitor at her place and more like he belonged there. "I'm sorry, sweetheart, but I had something I needed to tell you. How you doing?" he asked, hugging her and kissing her on the cheek.

As they sat down in the living room, Jelisa was puzzled by his sudden visit and curious about whatever it was he needed to say. She was more concerned about leaving before Reggie caught up to her than anything. "I'm good, Donny. What's so important that you couldn't call me? You got me nervous. What's up?"

Donny was trying to find a way to say it without sounding so happy. "So I know it's none of my business, but do you know a girl named Chrissy?"

"Chrissy who? What's her last name?" Jelisa said, slightly irritated that he came over this late to ask her about another female. She rolled her eyes and checked the time on her watch before continuing, "Donny, seriously? It's almost midnight. Couldn't this have waited until tomorrow?"

Donny's attention was drawn to two suitcases sitting by the front door. "Well, by the looks of things, it seems like tomorrow would have been too late. You planning on going somewhere?"

Jelisa gave him that "duh" look. *This fool here. Why else would I have suitcases packed?* Ignoring his question, Jelisa said quickly, "What was it you needed to tell me, Donny? I don't have time for this. It's late."

"Oh, yeah, my bad. Chrissy, you know, the mixed one who used to live on the east side. I don't know her last name. But, you should know her. I mean, y'all have so much in common." He chuckled.

"Donny, does it look like I'm in the mood for this right now? You play too much. Go on and spit it out." Jelisa was beginning to become irritated, and the longer Donny kept her held up, the more time she lost.

"All right, all right. So, word is your boy, Shamar, got a baby with her. As a matter of fact, I think she's about the same age as your little girl. I just figured you should know that."

Right then, Jelisa's irritation turned into out-right anger. She snapped at him, saying, "Donny, are you serious right now? Did you really just come to me about some baby mama mess that has nothing to do with you?"

"Well, now, I wouldn't say it like that. You know I was trying to look out for you. For us."

Jelisa was irate. *Did he really just say us?* "Boy, are you serious right now? I swear you sound like a ho right now! What kind of man brings this kind of female drama to a woman? Huh? You got to be kidding me," she said under her breath.

Donny was embarrassed, and his pride was hurt by the way she spoke to him. He had no idea what she had been going through, so it took him completely by surprise.

"Donny, what the hell are you talking about 'us'? There is no us."

Donny stood to his feet and began pacing back and forth. "What you mean ain't no us? Are you crazy? I haven't been spending all this time with you 'cause I didn't have nothing else to do with my time! I thought we had something going here. How you gon' try to play me?" Donny pouted.

Apparently, he'd developed the illusion that Jelisa had genuine feelings for him. To her, that was definitely not the case, and she had no problem correcting his thinking. "Donny, get the hell out of here with that. You knew from the beginning that I wasn't trying to go there with you. What didn't you understand about that? Man, I am married; don't you get that?" Jelisa was past her boiling point. She wanted him out of her apartment and out of her life. She never expected for things to go this far.

Donny was just supposed to be a temporary fix to keep her mind off of Shamar. Somehow she lost sight of that, and now she was stuck trying to dig herself out of this hole. Donny was becoming furious with her toying with him. Standing before Jelisa was an insecure wannabe thug who had just had his pride crushed. As his eyes became moist, his face turned beet red. Donny had worn out his welcome and Jelisa was getting antsy.

"Look, Donny, you need to go. I don't have time to deal with this. Just leave. It was fun while it lasted, but there is nothing between us, okay?"

Not willing to be disrespected any longer, Donny stepped past Jelisa as if he was going to leave. Without warning, he spun around, backhanding her in the mouth. She belted out a scream as her head snapped back and blood spilled from her mouth. The force of the hit sent her flying across the room onto the floor. Donny was relentless in his assault as he hovered over her, pounding away at her face.

"Stop! Get off me!" she screamed repeatedly.

Suddenly, the door was kicked open and in the threshold stood Reggie. "Hey, young'un, anybody ever teach you not to put your hands on a lady?"

Donny was stunned and motionless as he stared into the barrel of a chrome .357. Before he could get a word out: bang! Fragments of Donny's head splattered on the wall.

"Oh my God!" Jelisa screamed as she jumped to her feet and tried to run to Mya's room.

Reggie tripped her, sending her crashing to the floor. "No, no, no, angel. Where do you think you're going? I don't get a thank-you or anything? Now how rude is that?"

"Oh my God, Reggie, don't do this!" she pleaded, struggling to stand to her feet.

All of the commotion had finally awakened Mya. As her daughter cried out, Jelisa's heart sank. She had to keep Reggie from turning his attention to Mya. This meant she would have to give him what he wanted.

"Jelisa, I told you we didn't have to do this the hard way; but I guess you learned to like it rough." He laughed.

"All right, Reggie, I'll do whatever you want. Please don't hurt my baby!" she cried.

"Finally, you're starting to come to your senses. But we'll take care of that later. I guess it's a good thing you are already packed. Unless you plan on explaining this body to the law, you might want to pack up baby girl and come with me."

Jelisa knew he was right. With her track record, the police were sure to put that body on her. As much as she didn't want to do it, she had no other choice. She went and grabbed Mya from her room and put her coat on her. By now, the lakefront air was nippy as the temperature was dropping. Police sirens played in the background as they packed their things into Reggie's trunk. They loaded the car and sped off down the road, barely missing the police. Jelisa had no idea where they were going. As she pulled her coat closed, she remembered that she had tucked her pistol in the pocket earlier. At least now she had some sense of security.

The next morning, Shamar decided to finally go and settle things with Jelisa. When he turned onto her street, there were police cars and yellow tape everywhere. Immediately, worry invaded his mind, and he found it hard to breathe. He slammed on his brakes and threw the car into park when he realized the police were in front of Jelisa's house. Shamar jumped out of the car and ran toward the apartment.

"No! Jelisa! Jelisa! Where is my wife and my daughter?!" he yelled as the police restrained him.

"Sir, please calm down. Do you live here?" one of the officers said.

"Man, get the hell off me! Where is my wife?" Shamar barked at the cop.

"Sir, are you related to the victim?"

"What victim? Oh my God, man, come on! Fam, where is my family? Stop asking me all these questions."

"Are you related to a Donald Strong, sir?"

Shamar was confused; he didn't know anyone named Donald. "Man, I don't know who you're talking about. Where is my wife, Jelisa?"

The officer showed him Donny's picture and everything started to make sense. But where were Jelisa and Mya? When he realized that Donny was the victim, Shamar turned and walked off, heading to his car.

"Sir, do you know this gentleman? Sir, come back here!" the officer shouted.

Shamar looked back and replied, "Man, I don't know no Donald. I have to find my wife!" He got in the car and drove off, heading toward Sandra's house, hoping she was there. He frantically tried calling Jelisa's cell, but it kept going to voice mail.

Racing down the road, blowing through stop signs, Shamar made it to Sandra's house in minutes. The tires screeched as the car came to a halt in front of her house. He got out and ran up to the front door. He pounded on the door repeatedly, and Sandra came to the door with panic on her face.

"Who the hell is this banging on my door?" she asked as she swung the door open. She was shocked to see Shamar on the other side. Just as she began to smile at this sight, she was unnerved by the look on Shamar's face. He stood there breathing heavy and sweating profusely. "Shamar, what are you doing here? When did you get back?"

"Hey, Sandra, have you seen Jelisa and Mya?" he asked, struggling to get his words out.

"No, I haven't seen or heard from her since yesterday. Baby, what's wrong? You're scaring me."

Shamar entered the house and made his way into the living room, where Shawnie was sitting. "Hey, Shawnie, how you doing? Have you seen or heard from Jelisa? Something happened at her apartment, and nobody can tell me anything. I need some answers."

Shawnie had a confused look painted on her face. "Shamar, I don't know. I haven't heard from her since yesterday. Did you try calling her?"

"Of course I did!" he snapped. "This can't be happening right now."

Shawnie sat up and moved to the edge of her seat. "Shamar, what are you talking about? What happened?"

Shamar covered his face with his hands, wiping off the sweat. "I don't know, Shawnie. They found that fool Donny laid out at her apartment. There was blood everywhere, and Jelisa is nowhere to be found. This here is crazy, man. What the hell has she been doing while I was gone? Shawnie, that's your sister; you've got to know something," Shamar begged her for some answers.

"Shamar, um, look, I hate to tell you this, but Jelisa and Donny were creeping. That's all I know, I swear. I guess that was why he was over there, but I hope Jelisa didn't do it. Let me try to call her." Shawnie tried calling, but she too got Jelisa's voice mail. "Mama, why are you just sitting there? Have you heard from Jelisa?"

Sandra sat in silence, contemplating.

"Sandra? Sandra? Do you know something we don't?" Shamar asked, tapping her on the leg.

"I don't know nothing, but I'm sure going to find out." Sandra got up and grabbed her coat and car keys.

"Mama, what are you doing? Where are you going?" Shawnie yelled. Sandra didn't respond; she just stormed out. The next thing the two of them heard were her tires screaming as she drove off.

In her mind, Sandra always knew this day would come. She had a strong feeling that Reggie had something to do with Jelisa disappearing. Regret set in as she thought back to the day that her daughter tried to tell her what Reggie had done to her.

That morning, she went into Jelisa's room to wake her up for school. When she opened the door, she found her and Shamar fast asleep in the bed. She went ballistic at the sight of them, as she had always had her reservations about him. The thought of her child being in love with this gang-banging dope boy turned her stomach. Sandra wouldn't have it; she protested against their relationship from the first day Jelisa brought him home. She felt so disrespected looking at the two teens curled up under Jelisa's comforter.

Sandra went in to the kitchen and grabbed a pitcher of ice cold water out of the refrigerator. She returned to the room furious and, without thinking twice, she doused the both of them. Simultaneously, the couple jumped out of bed in shock.

"Mama, what are you doing? Oh my God, seriously?" Jelisa screamed as water and chills ran down her back.

"How dare you bring that bastard in my house without my permission? Get the hell out of my house now!" she shouted.

Shamar was speechless. Soaking wet, he hurried and gathered his things and ran out of the house.

Sandra stood over Jelisa, breathing heavy with her hands on her hips. "Little girl, you have a lot of nerve bringing that hood into my house. So now you think you're grown, huh? You having sex in my house?"

As Sandra laid into her, Jelisa sat silently with her head down in shame. Not because of what her mother was saying, but because she obviously had no clue the kind of torment she had just endured the night before.

"Don't just sit there looking stupid, answer me! Why would you have him in my house?"

Jelisa held back as long as she could until she finally broke. "Mama, why don't you ask Reggie?"

"What's that supposed to mean?" Sandra countered, offended at what she was suggesting.

"Mama, if you don't know, then nothing I say is going to make any difference. Just forget about it."

Sandra knew what Jelisa was referring to. But she was so in love with Reggie and afraid of losing him that she wouldn't allow herself to believe he was capable of hurting her child.

From that point on, Jelisa resented her mother. And when she found out she was pregnant, she was happy that she finally had someone to love her unconditionally. The news of her pregnancy solidified her and Shamar's relationship but caused a permanent rift between her and Sandra.

As Sandra journeyed down memory lane, her dreaming was interrupted by the blaring of car horns from the people behind her at a stop sign. She continued driving, heading to the one place she figured Reggie would be if he did indeed have something to do with Jelisa disappearing.

Shamar left Sandra's house hell-bent on finding his family. He drove to the west side to meet up with Block and Tamika, hoping they would be able to help. When he turned the corner onto Willard Avenue, he could see Block's Chevy parked near Pullman Field. It was close to noon. Block stepped out of the car and greeted Shamar with a handshake and head nod.

"What's good, homie? I hear you got problems," Block said, standing with his arms folded and leaning against a telephone pole.

"Man, Block, everything is crazy right now. They found ol' boy Donny with his head blown all over Jelisa's apartment. Worse than that, I can't reach her. I don't know if something happened to her and my daughter or what. Hell, for all I know, he came after her, and she did him in. Either way it goes, bruh, I need to find out something. Block, tell me something," he pleaded.

"Bro, you know I got you. I told you the other day that I was going to hold you down. My connect on the south side hit me with the business about this cat from out of town cruising around here in a black Cadillac. I don't have a name, but my guy said you can't miss him; he sticks out like a sore thumb. It's a long black old-school 'Lac with blacked-out windows. I don't know if that helps, but they say he's holing up at the ABC Motel, so I would check there first."

Shamar nodded and gave Block some dap. "All right, bet! Check it out, though. I need to hold some heat."

"Say no more. I got you," Block said, motioning for Shamar to follow him to the back of the car. He popped the trunk and looked at Shamar with a smirk. "Whatever you need, homie. Pick your poison."

Shamar didn't hesitate, choosing from the small arsenal Block had tucked in a black duffel. After grabbing a black 9 mm, he stashed it under his hoodie and thanked Block. They bid each other good-bye.

Block called out as Shamar walked toward his car, "Holla at me if you need me, homie. Be safe!"

"All right, fam!" Shamar jumped back in his car and sped off, jumping on the highway as time was quickly ticking away.

Reggie and Jelisa had arrived at a run-down motel on the south side early that morning. It was usually inhabited by pimps and drug addicts; so, besides his car, Reggie was not likely to stick out.

As he hurried Jelisa and Mya into the room he had been renting, Jelisa was terrified. Not knowing what was next to come tormented her. All she could think about was keeping Mya safe. She wished that Shamar was there to rescue them. The longer she sat in that nasty hotel room, the more she regretted ever stepping out on Shamar. She and that slut karma were about to have it out, especially if she didn't figure out how to get out of this situation.

Reggie jumped in the shower while she fed Mya a Lunchables that she'd picked up from a gas station on the way there. When they stopped, Reggie never let her out of his sight. If she had even thought of trying something, he had a trump card: he made her leave Mya in the car with him. She hadn't slept much. It was nearly impossible knowing the Reggie was there watching the whole time.

While he showered, Jelisa took her phone from the coat pocket she had hidden it in while she was getting Mya ready to leave the apartment. Jelisa didn't want the police involved for fear that things would fall back on her. Neither did she want to involve her sisters. She didn't want that on her conscience. She secretly sent out a distress message to someone she knew would be able to help her out of this jam. Just before Reggie emerged from the bathroom, Jelisa turned the phone off and put it back into her coat pocket. He came out with a towel wrapped around his waist.

"You've been behaving yourself, I hope. Wouldn't want anything to happen to my little angel," he said, caressing her cheek with the back of his hand.

Jelisa flinched and leaned away from him, disgusted by his presence. "Reggie, why don't you just let me go? I promise I won't say anything to anybody. I just need to get away from here. I swear to God, I'll give you whatever you ask for," Jelisa pled for her and her daughter's lives.

Reggie just laughed and went back into the bathroom to get dressed. Although he had every intention to get what he wanted from her, he wouldn't dare do it in front of her daughter.

When Reggie reappeared from the bathroom, he stood in the doorway, rubbing his hands together and licking his lips. "So, angel, what shall we do today? You know you've probably got every cop in the city looking for you? This might be our last dance, and I'm sure going to enjoy it."

Jelisa couldn't take it anymore; something had to be done. She reached over to a nearby chair where her coat hung. Reggie walked over to the full-length mirror that hung on the wall to adjust his tie. This was her chance; his back was turned, and he was consumed with his image staring back at him. Jelisa slid her hand into the pocket and pulled out her pistol, tucking it under her shirt.

Noticing her movement out of the corner of his eye, Reggie toyed with her to push her to reveal what she was concealing. He turned back toward her and slowly walked her way. "You know something, I was thinking we should just bypass all of the formalities and dip off into the bathroom. You can go ahead and take care of your debt, and little mama don't have to see or hear anything. What do you say?" he asked as he inched closer to her.

With every step he took, Jelisa's adrenaline pumped faster. As he got within a foot of her, she gently pushed Mya's chair away from the table. Reggie caressed her cheek with his hand, also running his finger down to her chin. Just as he was about to kiss her lips, Jelisa reached under her shirt, placing the barrel of her pistol to his temple.

"Well, I see you've decided to play the odds, huh? What you plan on doing with that, love?"

Jelisa's hand trembled, and her eyes began to well up. Right then, her mind flashed back to her being raped. With every scene, she became more furious. Full of rage and hate, Jelisa let out a loud scream and pulled the trigger.

Click. Nothing happened. Click. Click. Again the gun didn't shoot.

Jelisa's eyes widened. She looked at the gun, and then back at Reggie with confusion on her face. Reggie grabbed her by the throat, picking her up off the ground. As Jelisa struggled with her legs dangling, Mya began to cry, terrified at what was happening. Just then, Reggie pinned her up against the wall, breaking the mirror.

"You little whore! Did you really think it was going to be that easy? You've obviously forgotten who I am." He fumbled around in his pants pocket with his free hand briefly and lifted it in a fist next to Jelisa's face. When she looked over at his hand, he opened it, dropping the bullets from her gun onto the floor. "You should probably sleep a little lighter," he said, throwing her onto the bed. "Now why'd you have to go and do that? Now you're going to make me take it from you."

Suddenly, there was a light knock at the door. "Housekeeping," a lady's voice said.

Reggie pulled out his pistol from behind his back in his waistline. He motioned for her to be quiet, putting his finger to his mouth. He slid the chair Mya was sitting in over to Jelisa and mouthed to her to keep her quiet.

As Reggie crept to the door, he called out, "Who is it?"

"Housekeeping, sir!" the lady responded.

Not wanting to draw any extra attention to their room, Reggie slowly opened the door. A beautiful young redbone stood before him in a hotel uniform and latex gloves with a cart full of cleaning supplies. She spoke quietly, saying,

"Hello, sir. I'm here to clean up a mess that was reported."

Reggie had an agitated look on his face, and he looked somewhat puzzled. "I'm sorry, baby girl, but there's no mess here. I think you might be mistaken." Reggie gave a fake smile and turned to look back at Jelisa. She covered Mya's eyes, looking at him with a dead stare. He asked, "Angel, you don't know anything about a mess, do you?"

She remained silent, and he turned back to the housekeeper, saying, "You see, there's no—"

Bang!

Mya screamed, and Jelisa jumped back, shielding her. As Reggie's face painted the walls, the woman dressed as a housekeeper stepped into the room, asking, "You okay, baby?" She dropped the gun, walked over to Jelisa, and helped her to her feet. Jelisa embraced her, and they shared a passionate kiss.

"What the hell?" Shamar said as he and Sandra stood in the doorway, both gasping for air. They arrived at the motel at the same time and had spotted Reggie's Cadillac.

"Jelisa, baby, what are you doing? What the hell happened here?" Sandra asked.

"Yeah, what the hell happened here?" Shamar added. "Hold up. Man, you gotta be kidding me right now. Chrissy, what are you doing here? Jelisa, how in the . . ." Shamar was completely confused. There, standing in front of him, were Jelisa and Chrissy kissing and hugging. This didn't make any sense. How did they know each other and why were they holding each other?

Chrissy smiled and mocked him, shooting a kiss at him from across the room.

Shamar reached down and grabbed the gun she had dropped, yelling, "Chrissy, I'm gonna—"

"You gonna do what, clown?" she interrupted, holding up a pink 9 mm.

Sandra stood there in shock. She looked over at Jelisa, who had a huge grin on her face. She was speechless, and she knew her daughter had to be behind this. "Jelisa, what did you do?"

"Mama, shut up!" Jelisa snapped back.

"I'ma kill you!" Shamar yelled, squeezing the trigger, but nothing happened.

"Now, now," Chrissy said. "I told you to leave me alone, didn't I? Now you two get over there!" she shouted, pointing for Shamar and Sandra to move toward the bathroom.

Shamar had a defeated look on his face. As he stared at Jelisa and Mya, all he could say was, "Why, Jelisa?"

She looked at him and, without any emotion, said, "This was never about you, Shamar. We just wanted a family, something my mother let this bastard take from me, and the thing you put everything before. I hate you. Now have fun trying to explain that body you just caught."

Chrissy pulled off the latex gloves she was wearing and tossed them at Shamar. He dropped the gun, and his heart dropped. "See you around, dummy," Chrissy said as they made their way past them and out the door.

As Jelisa and Chrissy sped off down the road, Shamar and Sandra could hear sirens screaming in the air.

"You go ahead and get out of here, Sandra. I'll take care of this."

Sandra hesitated; and, with tears streaming from her eyes, she looked at Shamar and said, "Baby, I'm so sorry. This is all my fault."

"Go! Get out of here!" Shamar shouted. He ran out behind her and headed to his car. He sped down Franklin Street and jumped on I-94 west, not knowing what he would do next.

After he made it through Illinois, he eased over to the outside lane. After he had wiped the gun clean, he threw it out the passenger window over the side of a bridge. Shamar holed up in a hotel somewhere in Iowa for a couple days.

After calling Block and filling him in about this situation, he told him to buy a train ticket to Arkansas, where he had a place for him to lie low. He figured the police would be looking for his car, so he ditched it at a rest stop and caught a cab to a nearby Amtrak station. As he boarded the train, Shamar was numb; he still couldn't believe Jelisa was setting him up this whole time. He still didn't know who the dead man in the hotel was, but one thing was for certain: Jelisa and Chrissy were going to pay.

Sandra blamed herself for everything that transpired that day. If she had listened when Jelisa tried to tell her about Reggie raping her, Jelisa's life never would have taken the turn it did.

Jelisa and Chrissy disappeared to the West Coast with their new family. They had Mya and Chrissy's two children; the family they had dreamed of was complete. So they vanished, without a trace. Not only had they both deceived Shamar by setting him up to take the fall for Reggie's murder, but they had also used him as a handpicked sperm donor. The plan they had hatched back before Jelisa was raped had finally come to fruition. With the life they wanted already set up, they knew their plan was so well crafted that Shamar would never come looking for them without putting himself at risk.

The war for Shamar hadn't ended in Iraq; it had just started. Now there was nothing but vengeance in his heart. He was now an army of one.